POKéMON

BLACK AND WHITE

VOL. 13

Story by **HIDENORI KUSAKA**
Art by **SATOSHI YAMAMOTO**

Pokémon
BLACK AND WHITE

Pokémon Black and White
Volume 13
VIZ Kids Edition

Story by HIDENORI KUSAKA
Art by SATOSHI YAMAMOTO

© 2013 Pokémon.
© 1995-2013 Nintendo/Creatures Inc./GAME FREAK inc.
TM, ®, and character names are trademarks of Nintendo.
POCKET MONSTERS SPECIAL (Magazine Edition)
by Hidenori KUSAKA, Satoshi YAMAMOTO
© 1997 Hidenori KUSAKA, Satoshi YAMAMOTO
All rights reserved.
Original Japanese edition published by SHOGAKUKAN.
English translation rights in the United States of America, Canada,
the United Kingdom and Ireland arranged with SHOGAKUKAN.

English Adaptation / Bryant Turnage
Translation / Tetsuichiro Miyaki
Touch-up & Lettering / Susan Daigle-Leach
Cover Art Assistance / Miguel Riebman
Design / Fawn Lau
Editor / Annette Roman

Printed in the U.S.A.

Published by VIZ Media, LLC
P.O. Box 77010
San Francisco, CA 94107

10 9 8 7 6 5 4 3 2 1
First printing, December 2013

Pokémon

BLACK and WHITE

VOL.13

Adventure 41
A LOST MELODY_____05

Adventure 42
THE BEGINNING_____29

Adventure 43
TOOTH AND CLAW_____49

Adventure 44
WELCOME HOME_____69

THE STORY THUS FAR!

Pokémon Trainer Black is exploring the mysterious Unova region with his brand-new Pokédex. Pokémon Trainer White runs a thriving talent agency for performing Pokémon. While traveling together, their paths cross with Team Plasma, a nefarious group that advocates releasing your Pokémon into the wild! Now Black and White are off on their own separate journeys of discovery...

BLACK'S dream is to win the Pokémon League!

WHITE'S dream is to make her Tepig Gigi a star!

Black's Munna, MUSHA, helps him think clearly by temporarily "eating" his dream.

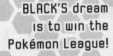

White's Tepig, GIGI, and Black's Emboar, BO, get along like peanut butter and jelly! But now Gigi has left White for another Trainer...

Adventure 41 A Lost Melody

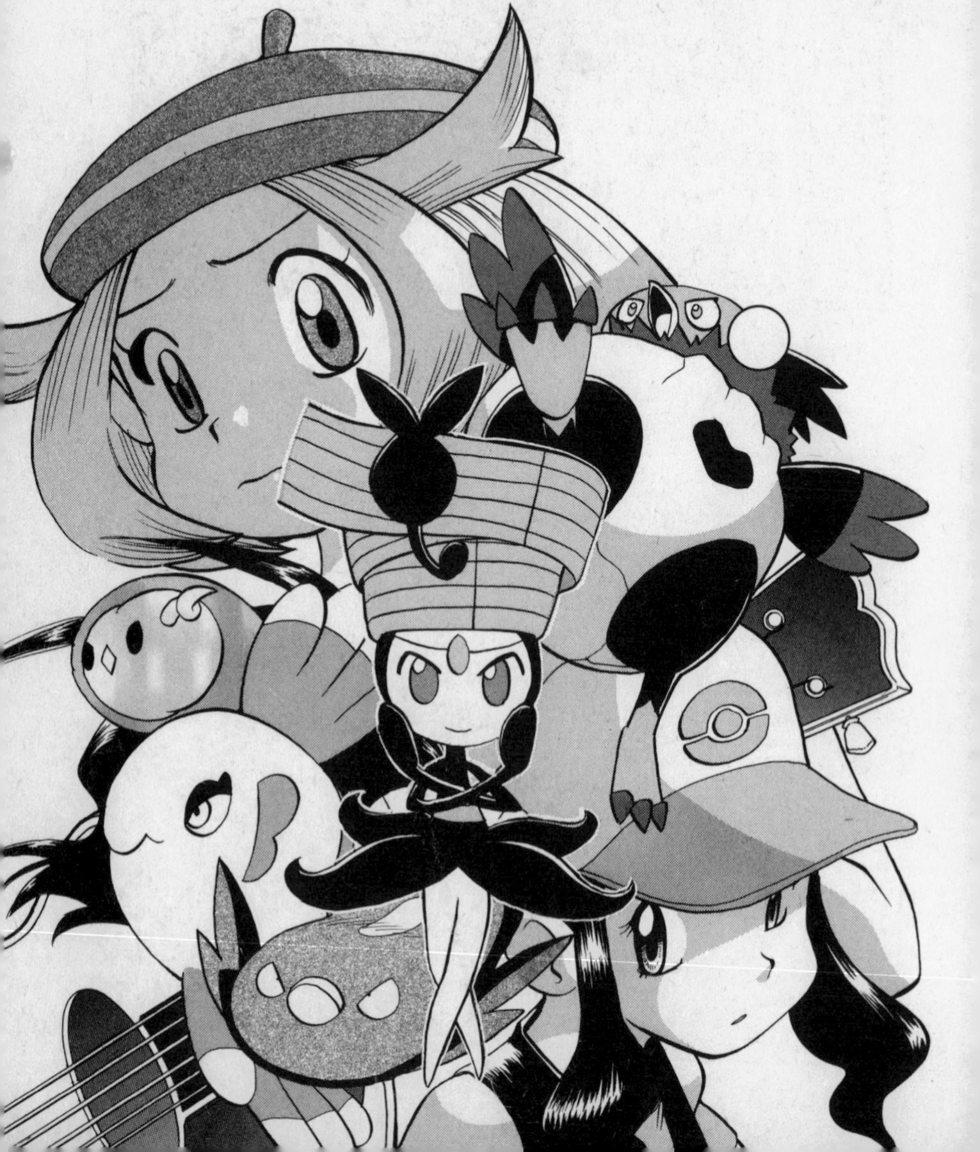

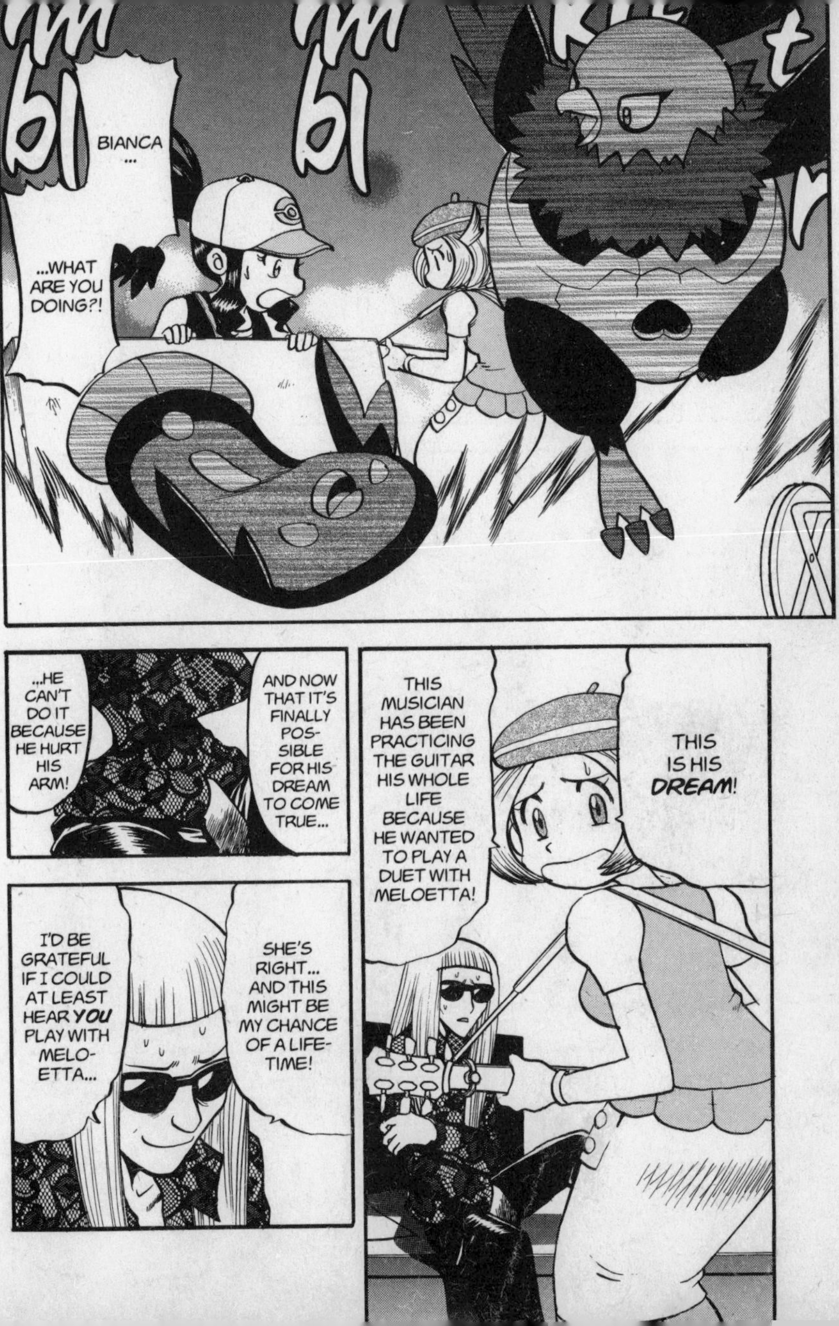
BIANCA ...
...WHAT ARE YOU DOING?!
THIS IS HIS DREAM!
THIS MUSICIAN HAS BEEN PRACTICING THE GUITAR HIS WHOLE LIFE BECAUSE HE WANTED TO PLAY A DUET WITH MELOETTA!
AND NOW THAT IT'S FINALLY POS-SIBLE FOR HIS DREAM TO COME TRUE...
...HE CAN'T DO IT BECAUSE HE HURT HIS ARM!
SHE'S RIGHT... AND THIS MIGHT BE MY CHANCE OF A LIFE-TIME!
I'D BE GRATEFUL IF I COULD AT LEAST HEAR YOU PLAY WITH MELO-ETTA...

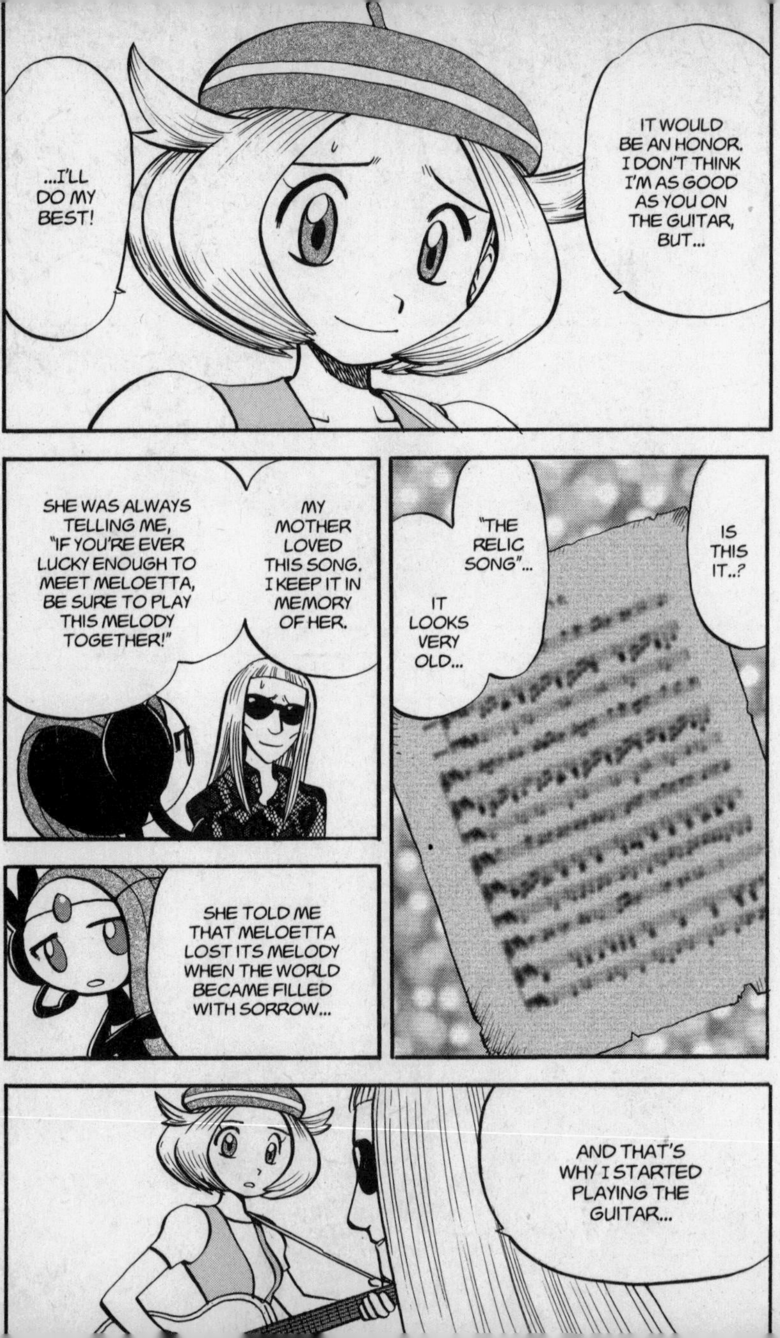
IT WOULD BE AN HONOR. I DON'T THINK I'M AS GOOD AS YOU ON THE GUITAR, BUT...
...I'LL DO MY BEST!
IS THIS IT..?
"THE RELIC SONG"...
IT LOOKS VERY OLD...
MY MOTHER LOVED THIS SONG. I KEEP IT IN MEMORY OF HER.
SHE WAS ALWAYS TELLING ME, "IF YOU'RE EVER LUCKY ENOUGH TO MEET MELOETTA, BE SURE TO PLAY THIS MELODY TOGETHER!"
SHE TOLD ME THAT MELOETTA LOST ITS MELODY WHEN THE WORLD BECAME FILLED WITH SORROW...
AND THAT'S WHY I STARTED PLAYING THE GUITAR...

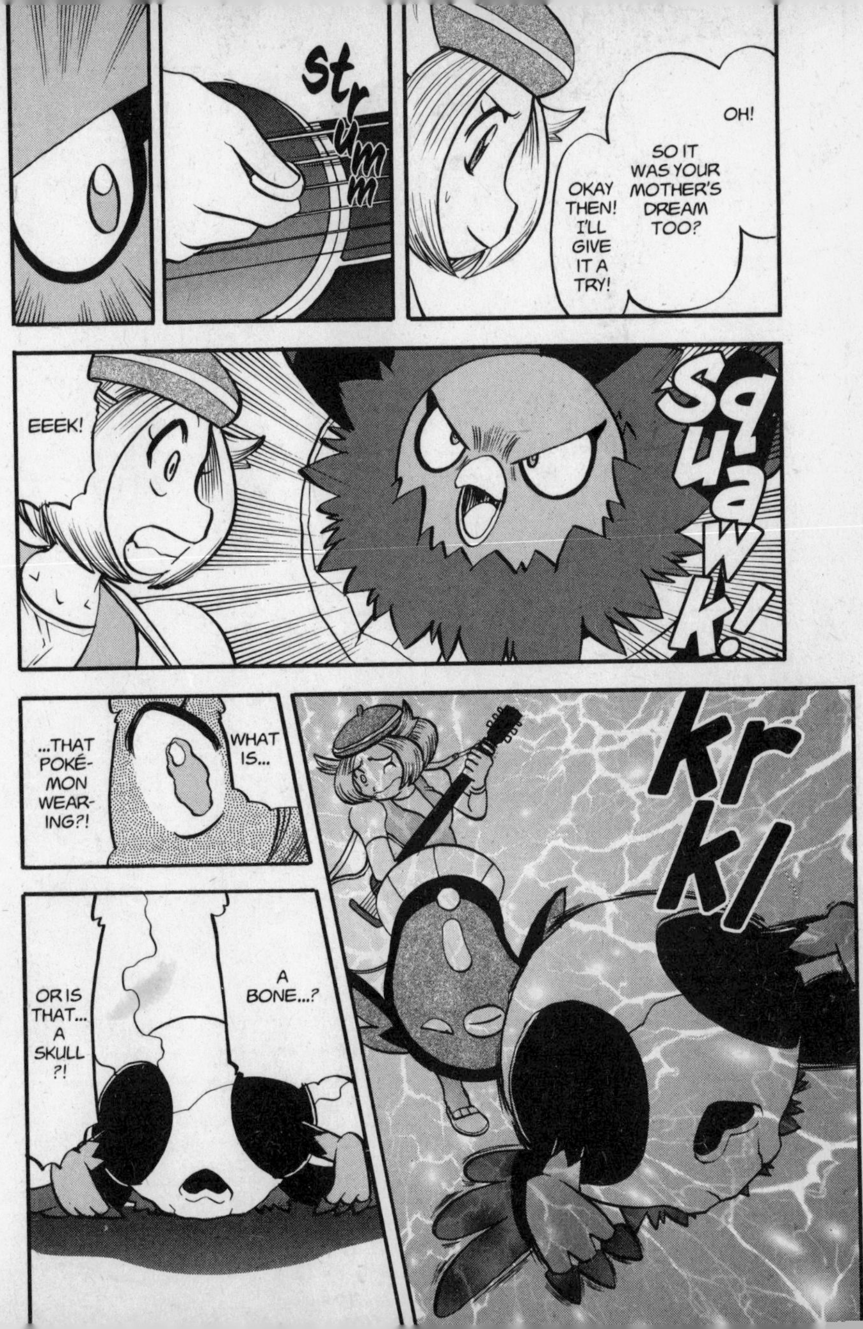
OH!
SO IT WAS YOUR MOTHER'S DREAM TOO?
OKAY THEN! I'LL GIVE IT A TRY!
strumm
squawk!
EEEK!
krkl
WHAT IS...
...THAT POKÉMON WEARING?!
A BONE...?
OR IS THAT... A SKULL?!

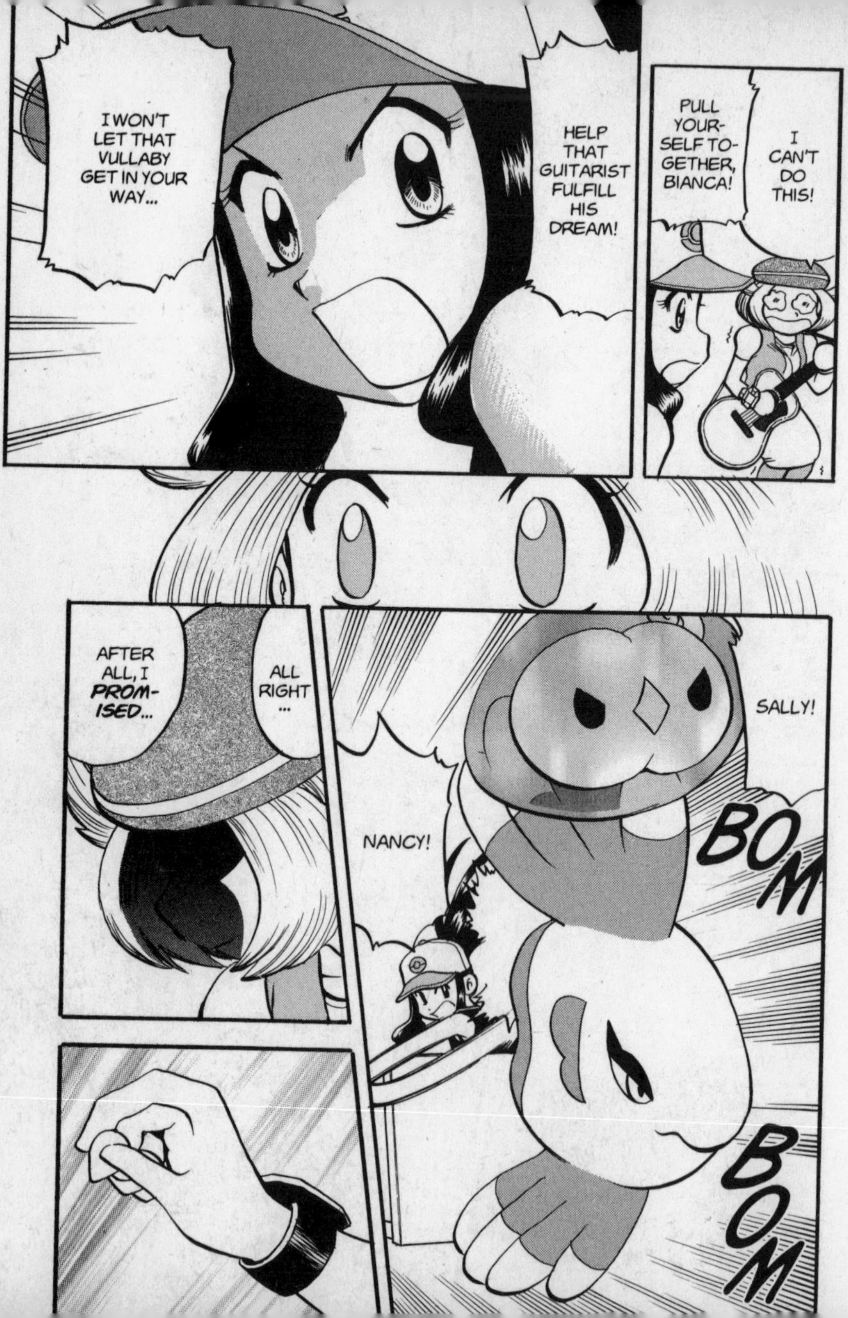
I CAN'T DO THIS!
PULL YOURSELF TOGETHER, BIANCA!
HELP THAT GUITARIST FULFILL HIS DREAM!
I WON'T LET THAT VULLABY GET IN YOUR WAY...
SALLY!
NANCY!
BOM
BOM
ALL RIGHT ...
AFTER ALL, I *PROMISED*...

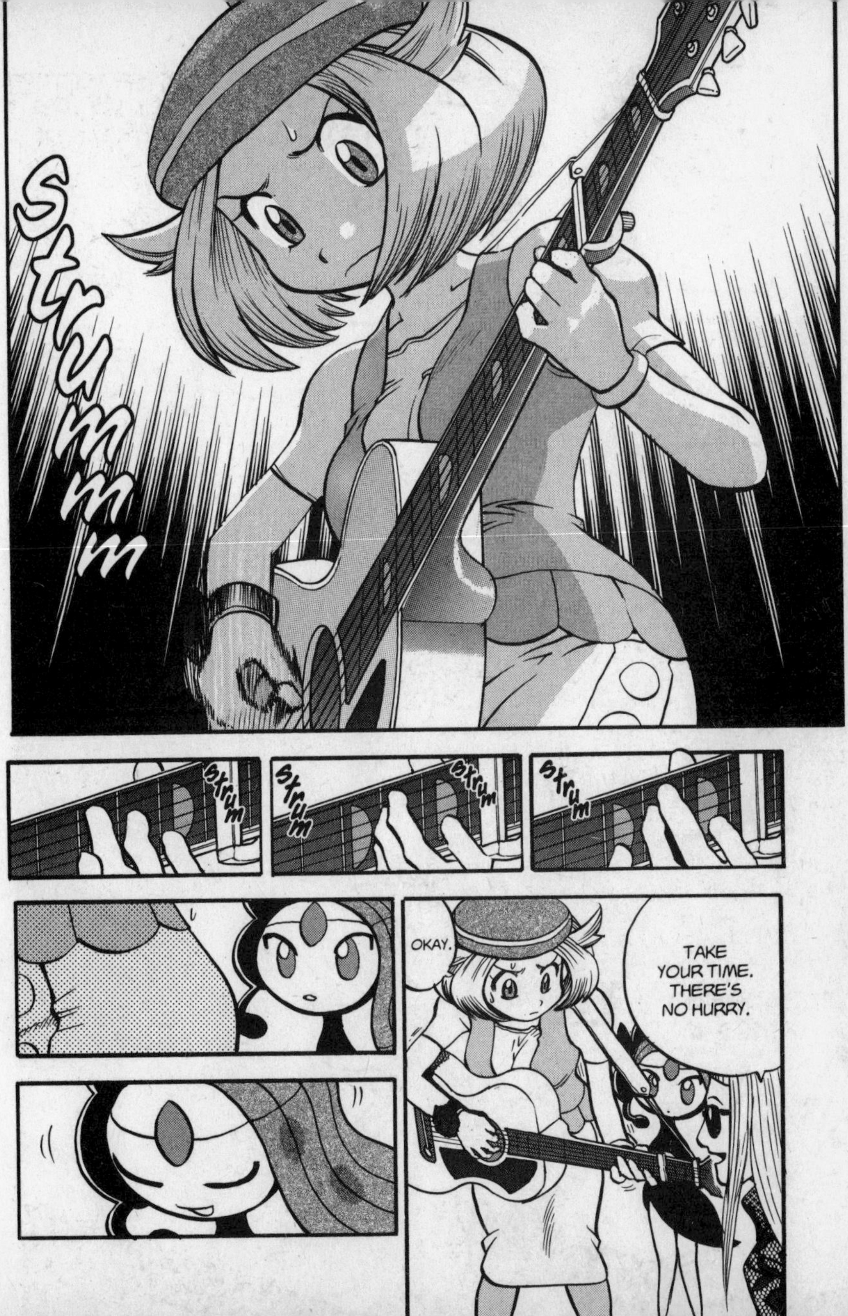
Strummm
strum
strum
strum
TAKE YOUR TIME. THERE'S NO HURRY.
OKAY.

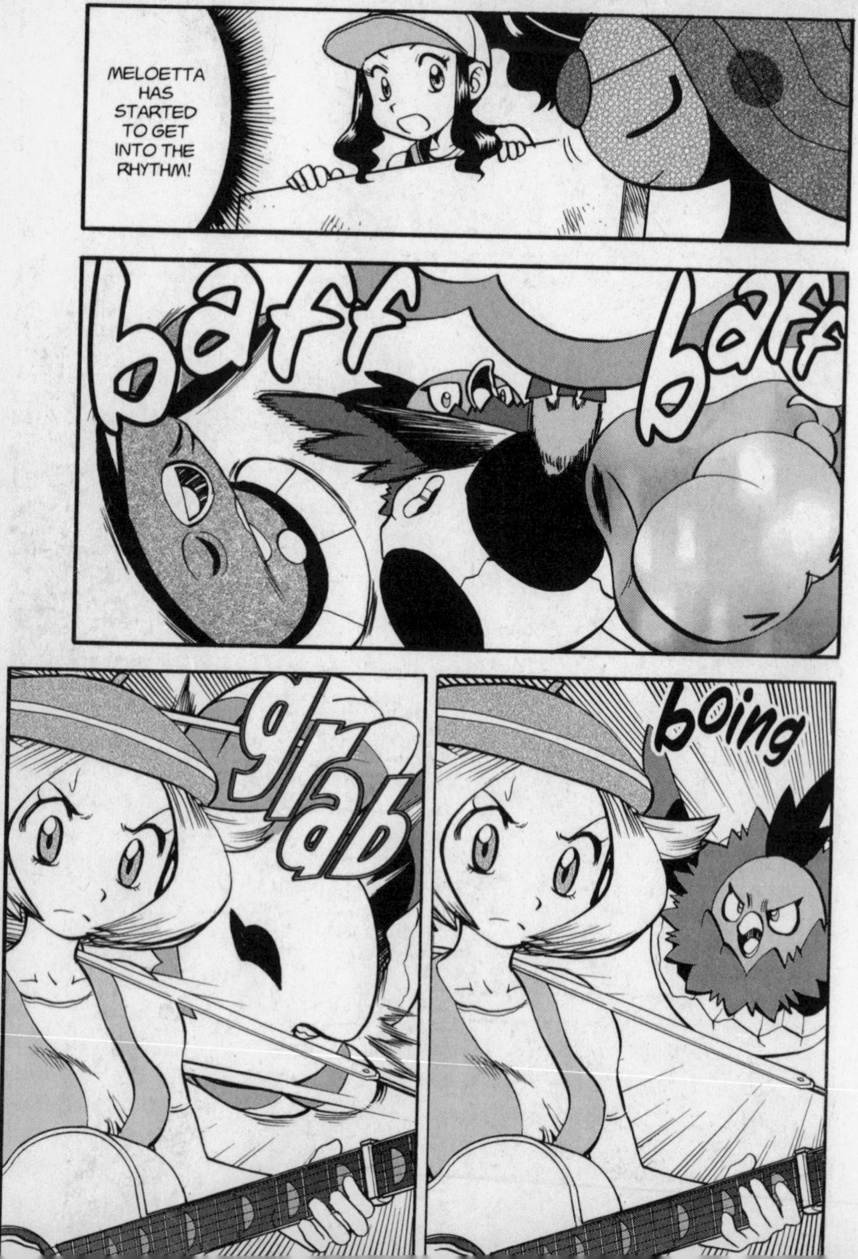
MELOETTA HAS STARTED TO GET INTO THE RHYTHM!
baff
baff
boing
grab

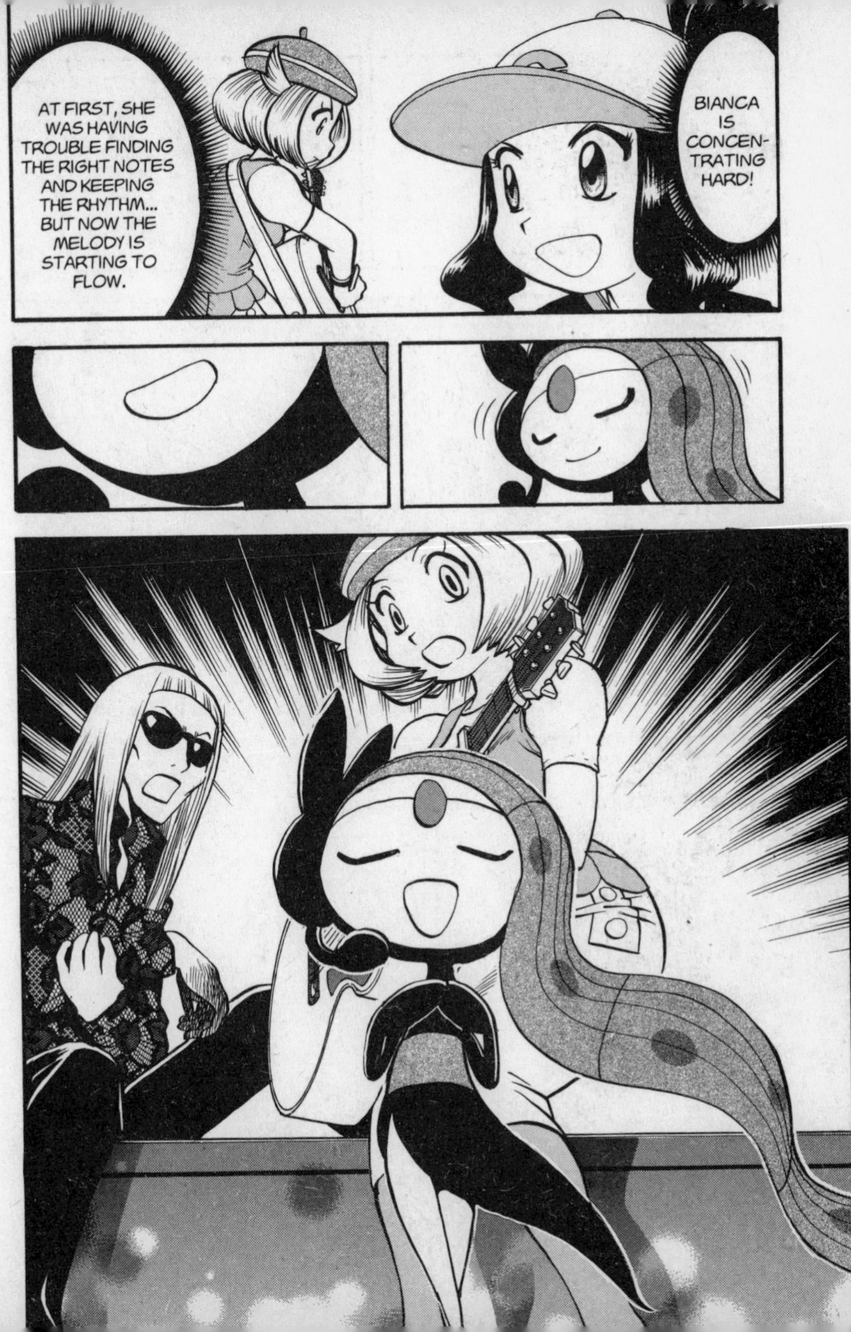
BIANCA IS CONCEN-TRATING HARD!
AT FIRST, SHE WAS HAVING TROUBLE FINDING THE RIGHT NOTES AND KEEPING THE RHYTHM... BUT NOW THE MELODY IS STARTING TO FLOW.

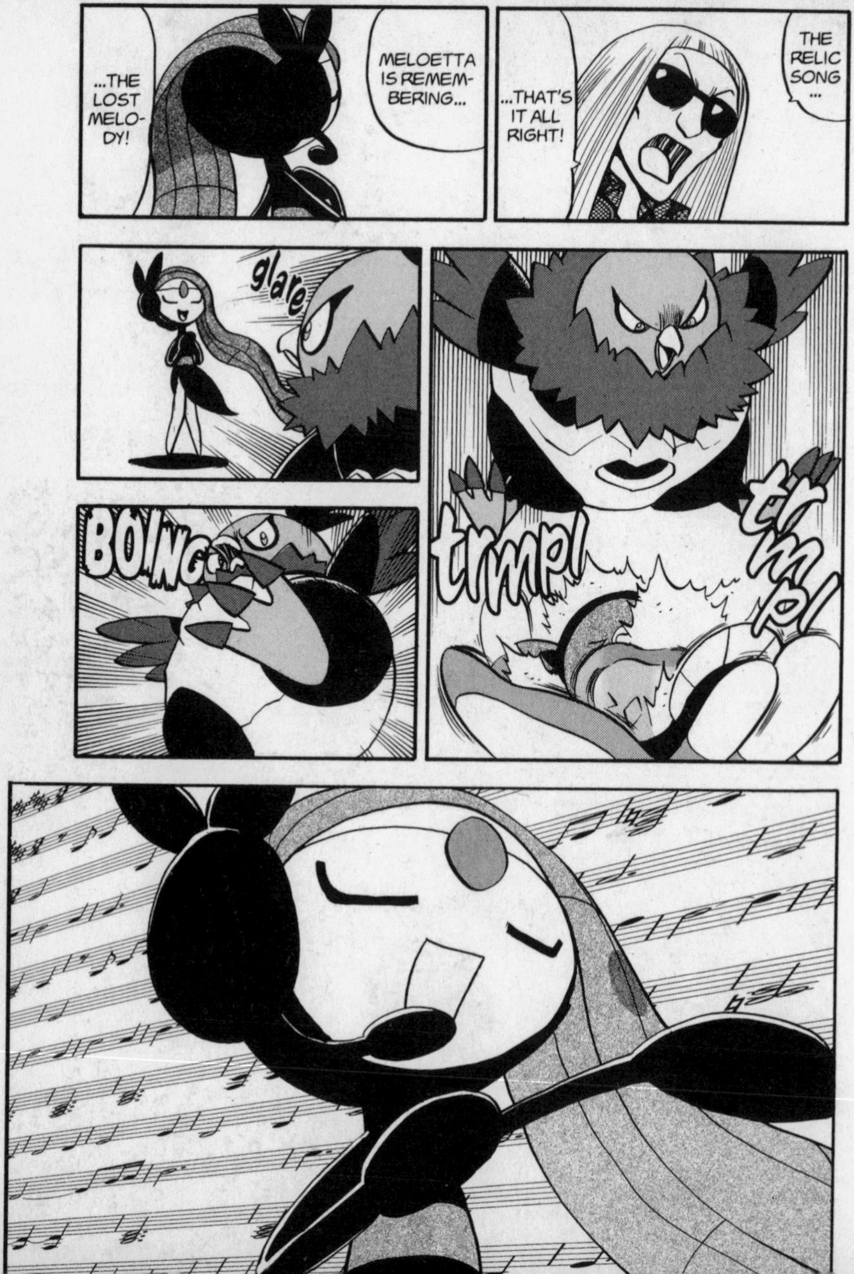
THE RELIC SONG ...
...THAT'S IT ALL RIGHT!
MELOETTA IS REMEMBERING...
...THE LOST MELODY!
trmpl
trmpl
glare
BOING

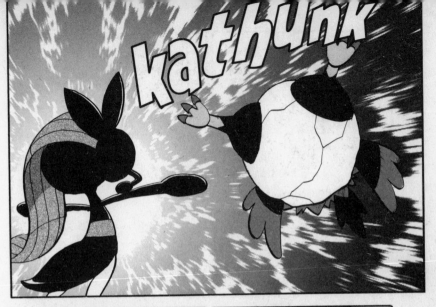

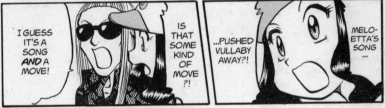

kathunk
MELO-ETTA'S SONG ...
...PUSHED VULLABY AWAY?!
IS THAT SOME KIND OF MOVE?!
I GUESS IT'S A SONG **AND** A MOVE!
IT'S ALL COMING BACK TO MELOETTA NOW THAT IT'S HARMONIZING WITH BIANCA!
strumm
strumm

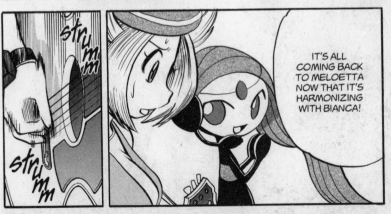

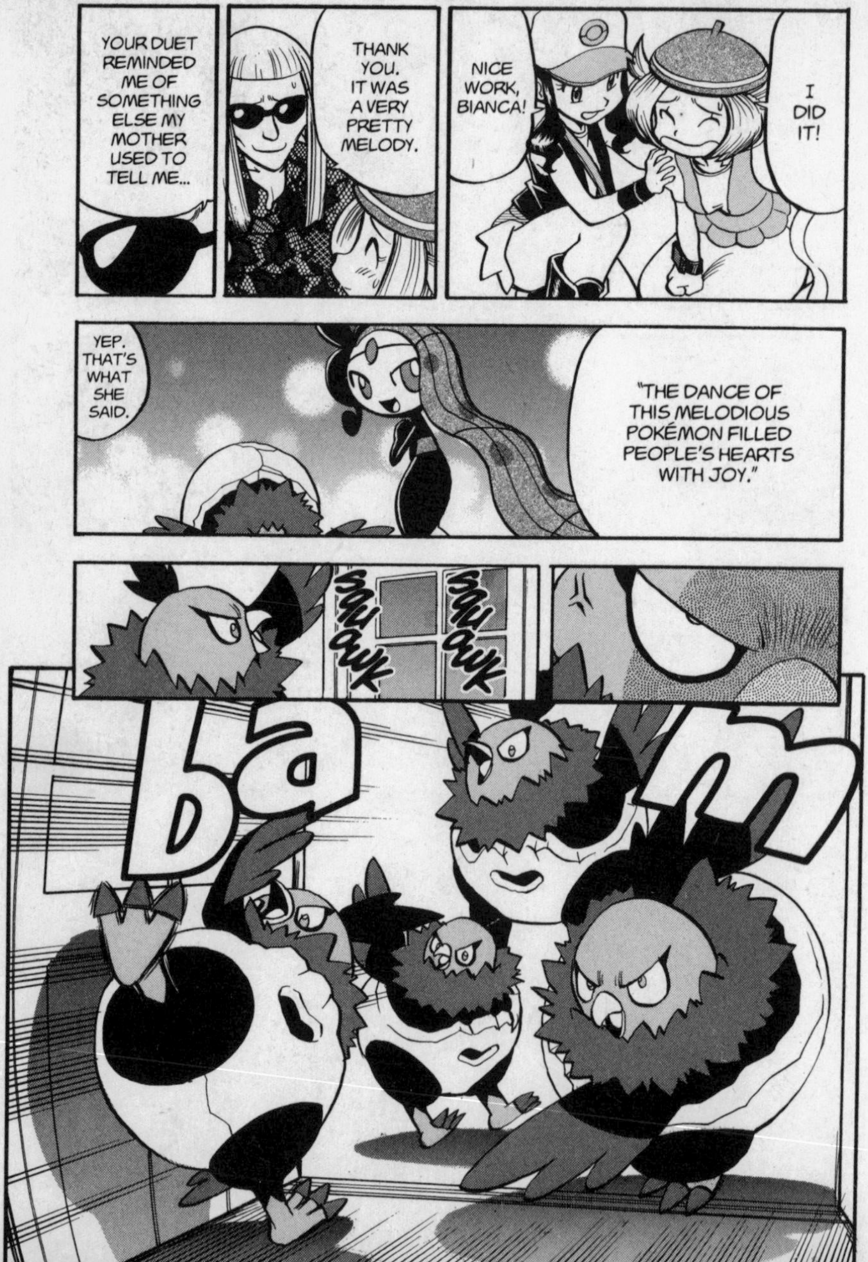
I DID IT!
NICE WORK, BIANCA!
THANK YOU. IT WAS A VERY PRETTY MELODY.
YOUR DUET REMINDED ME OF SOMETHING ELSE MY MOTHER USED TO TELL ME...
"THE DANCE OF THIS MELODIOUS POKÉMON FILLED PEOPLE'S HEARTS WITH JOY."
YEP. THAT'S WHAT SHE SAID.
squawk
squawk
bam

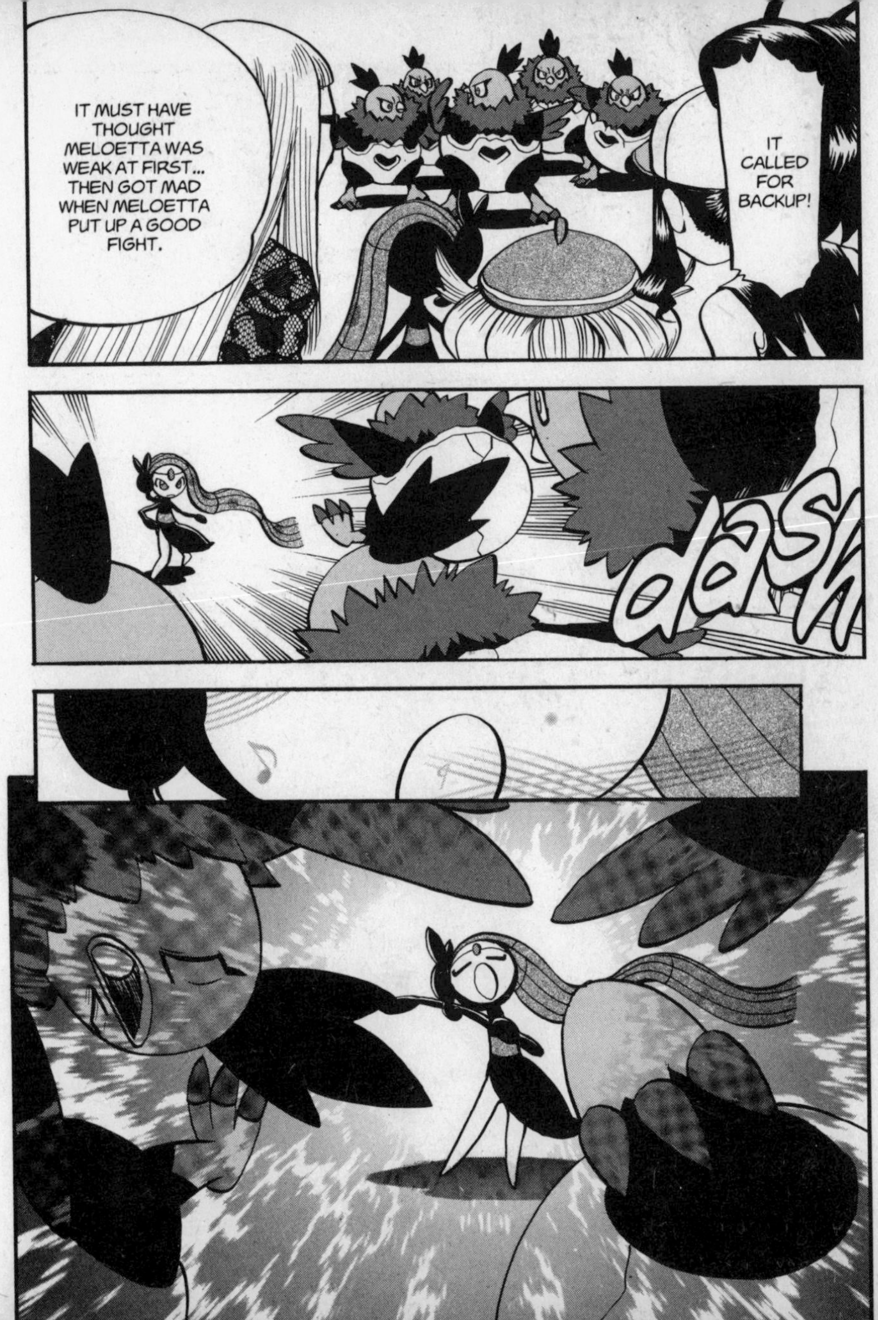
IT CALLED FOR BACKUP!
IT MUST HAVE THOUGHT MELOETTA WAS WEAK AT FIRST... THEN GOT MAD WHEN MELOETTA PUT UP A GOOD FIGHT.
dash

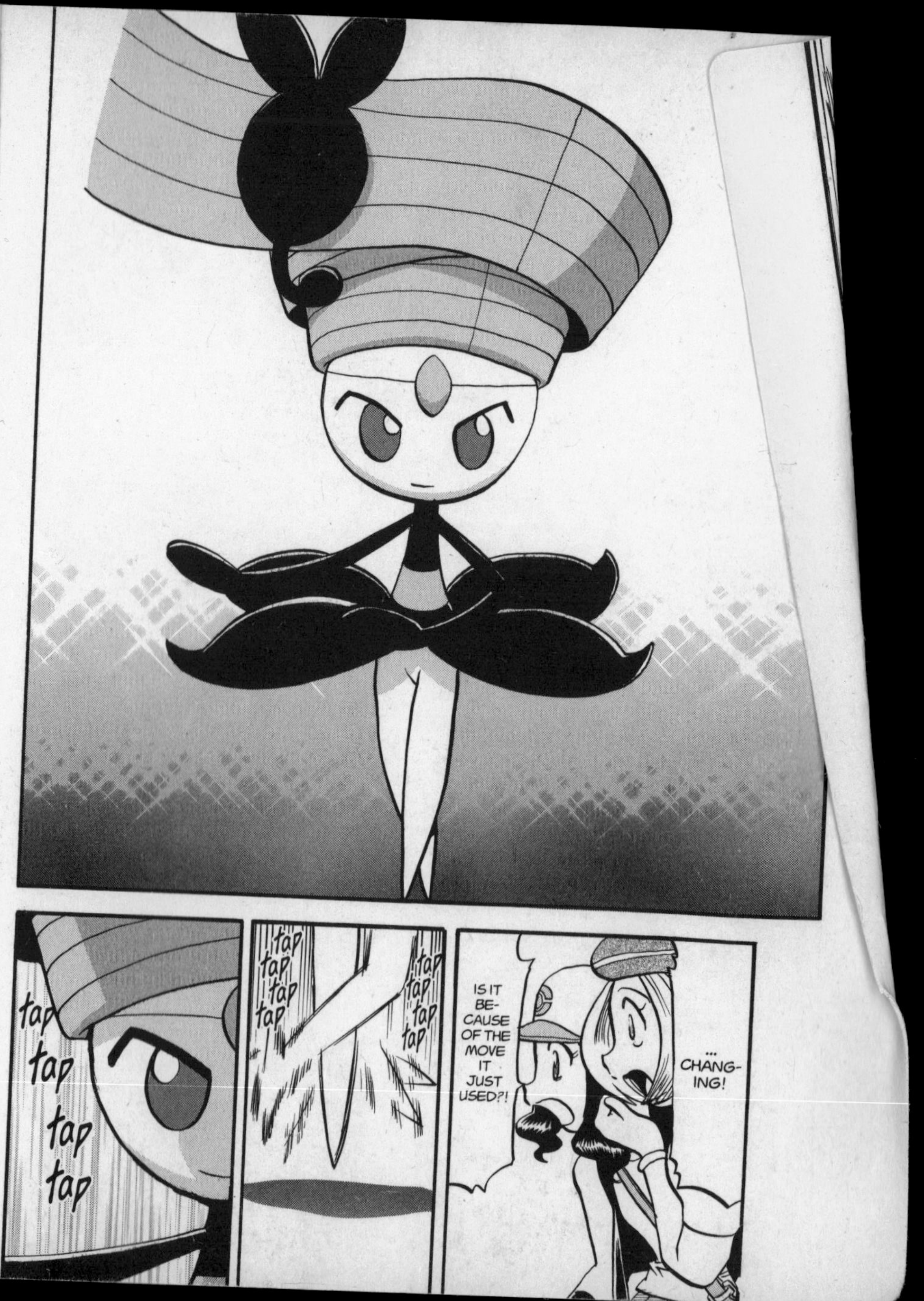
... CHANG-ING!
IS IT BE-CAUSE OF THE MOVE IT JUST USED?!
tap tap tap tap tap
tap tap tap tap
tap tap tap tap tap

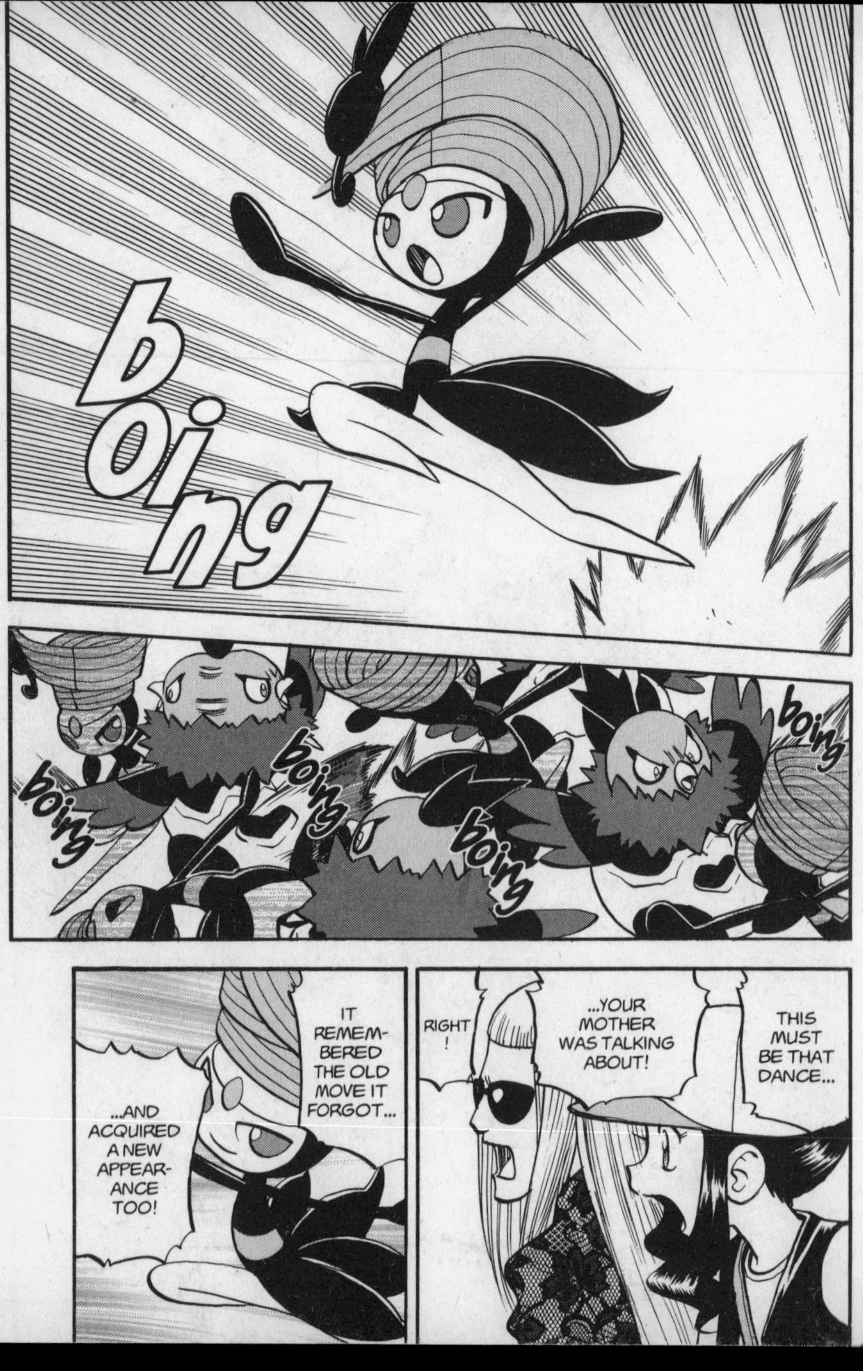
boing
boing
boing
boing
boing
THIS MUST BE THAT DANCE...
...YOUR MOTHER WAS TALKING ABOUT!
RIGHT!
IT REMEM-BERED THE OLD MOVE IT FORGOT...
...AND ACQUIRED A NEW APPEAR-ANCE TOO!

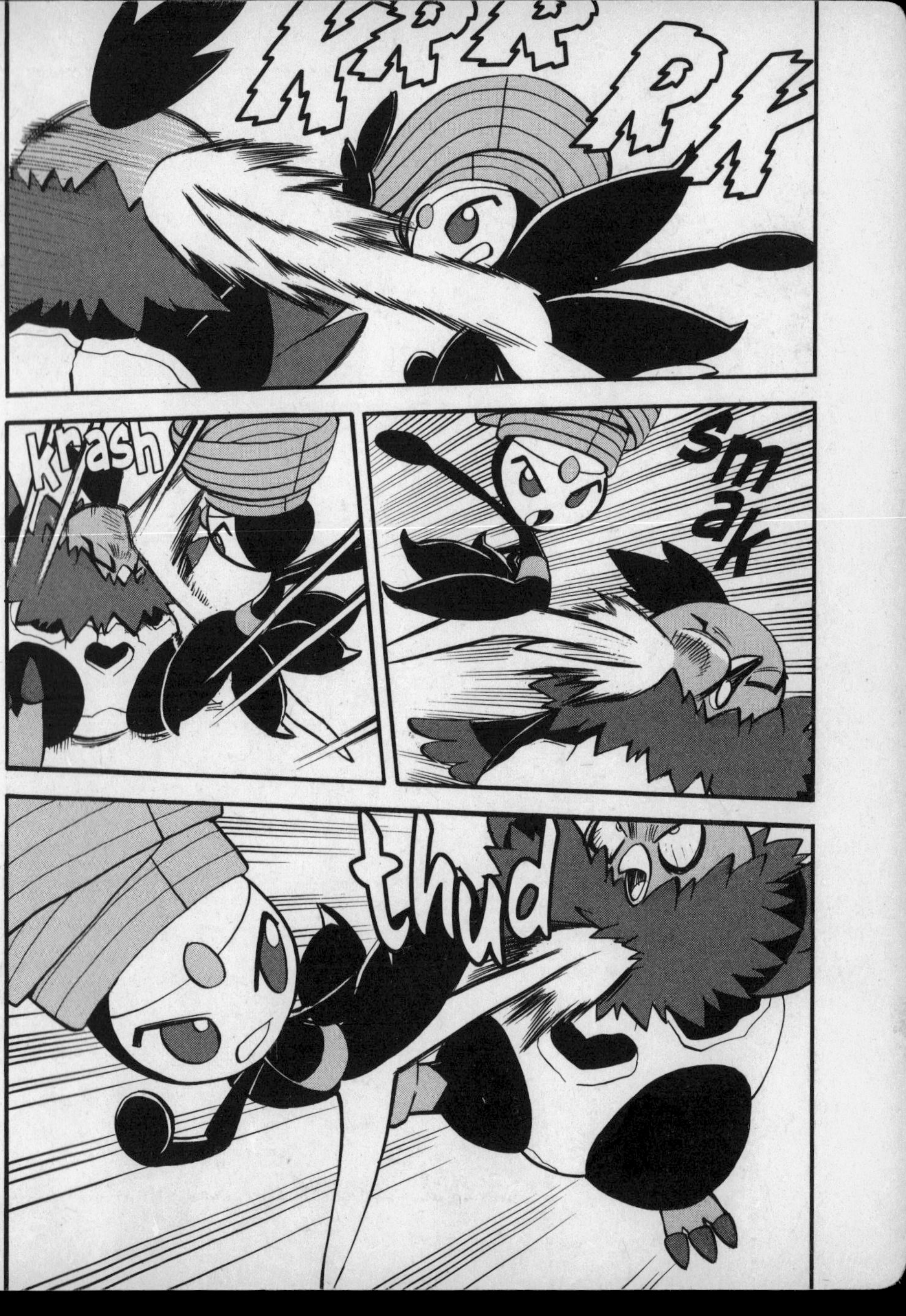
KRRRA
smak
krash
thud

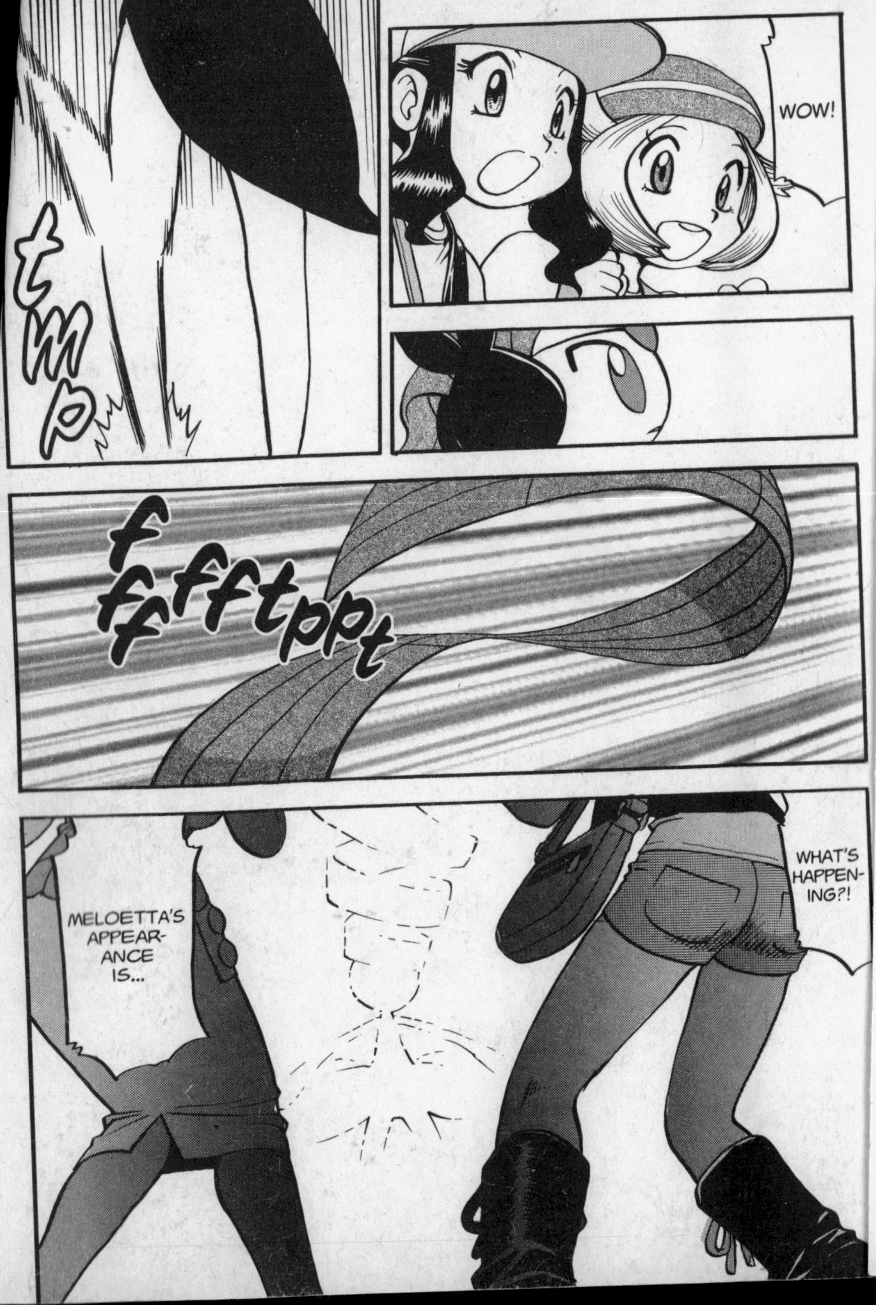
WOW!
tmp
ffffftppt
WHAT'S HAPPEN-ING?!
MELOETTA'S APPEAR-ANCE IS...

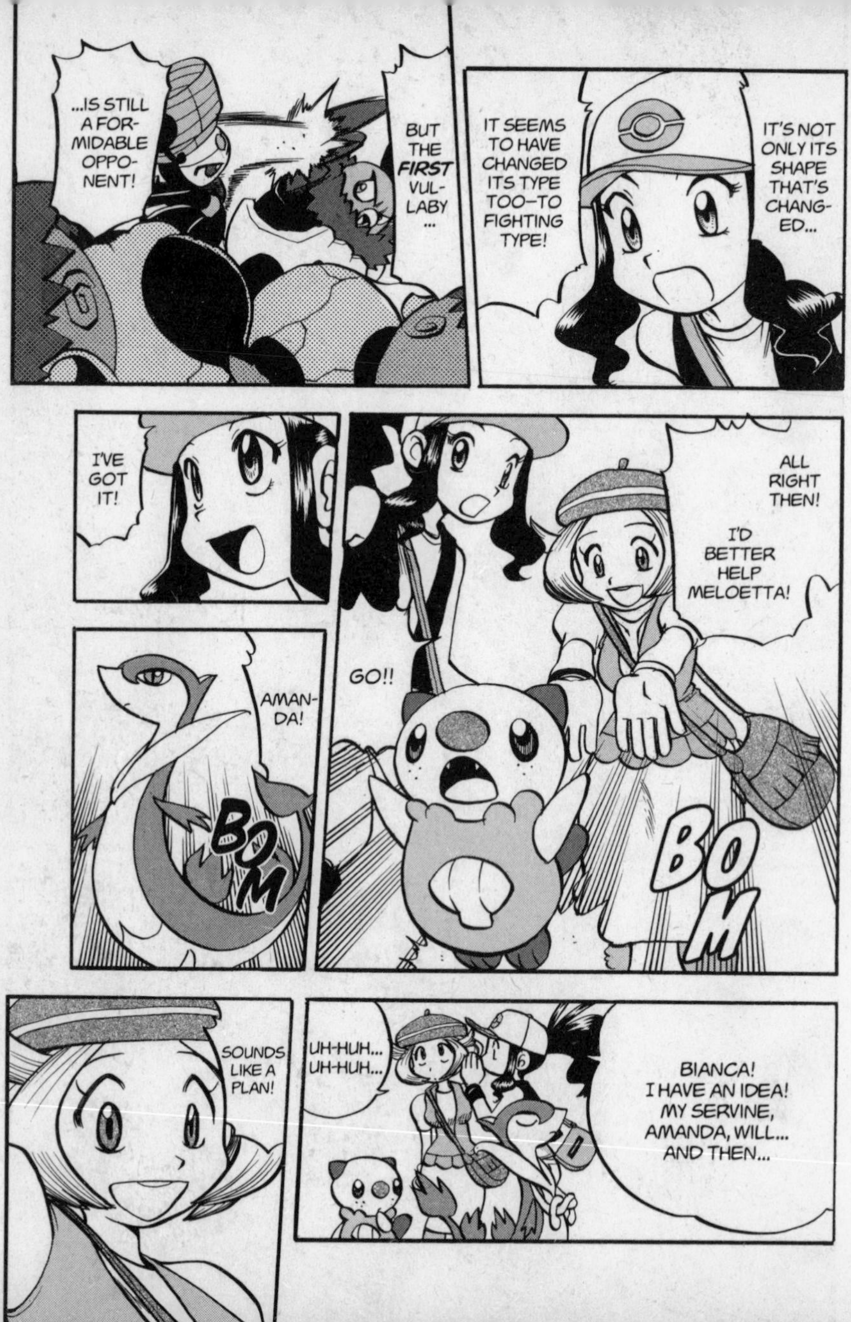
IT'S NOT ONLY ITS SHAPE THAT'S CHANGED...
IT SEEMS TO HAVE CHANGED ITS TYPE TOO—TO FIGHTING TYPE!
BUT THE *FIRST* VULLABY...
...IS STILL A FORMIDABLE OPPONENT!
ALL RIGHT THEN!
I'D BETTER HELP MELOETTA!
GO!!
BOM
I'VE GOT IT!
AMANDA!
BOM
BIANCA! I HAVE AN IDEA! MY SERVINE, AMANDA, WILL... AND THEN...
UH-HUH... UH-HUH...
SOUNDS LIKE A PLAN!

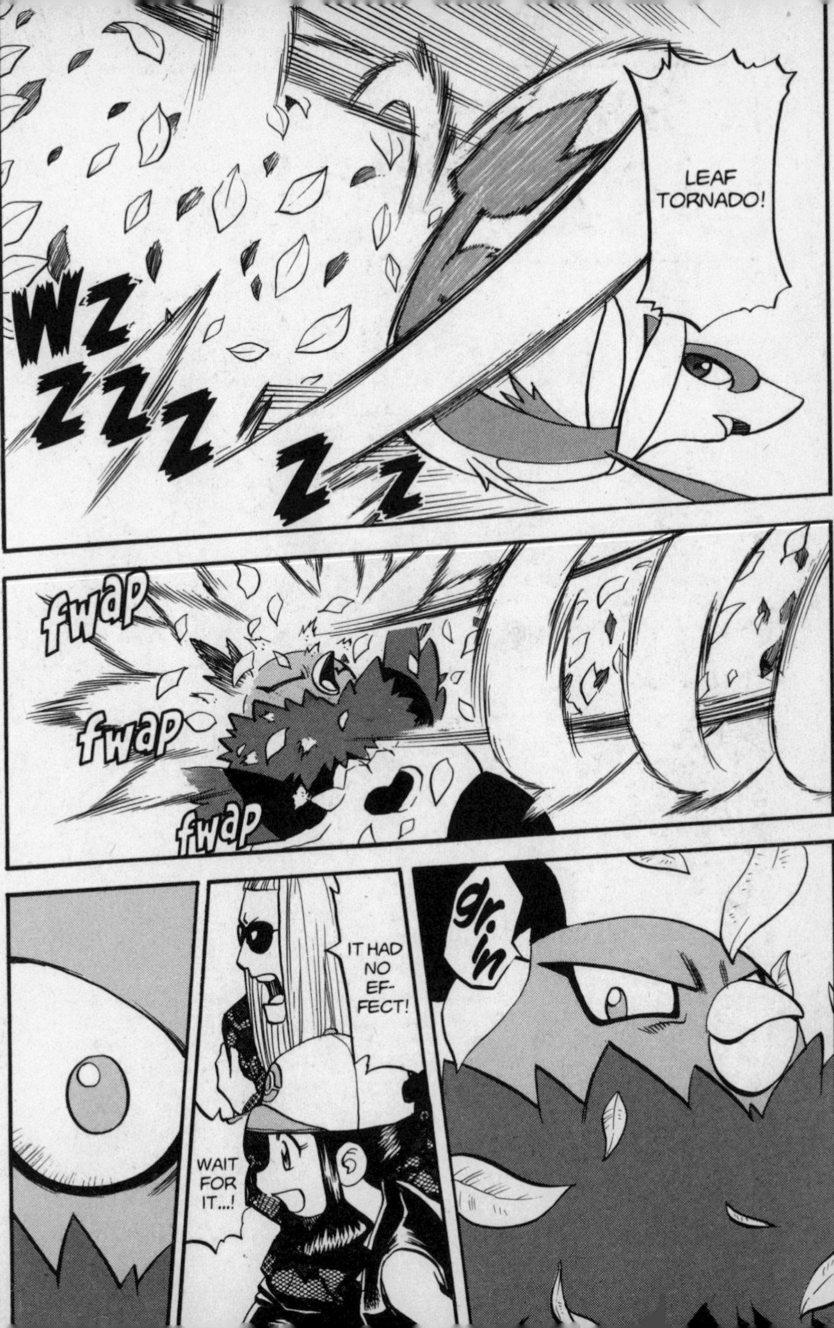
LEAF TORNADO!
WZZZZZZ
fwap
fwap
fwap
grin
IT HAD NO EF-FECT!
WAIT FOR IT...!

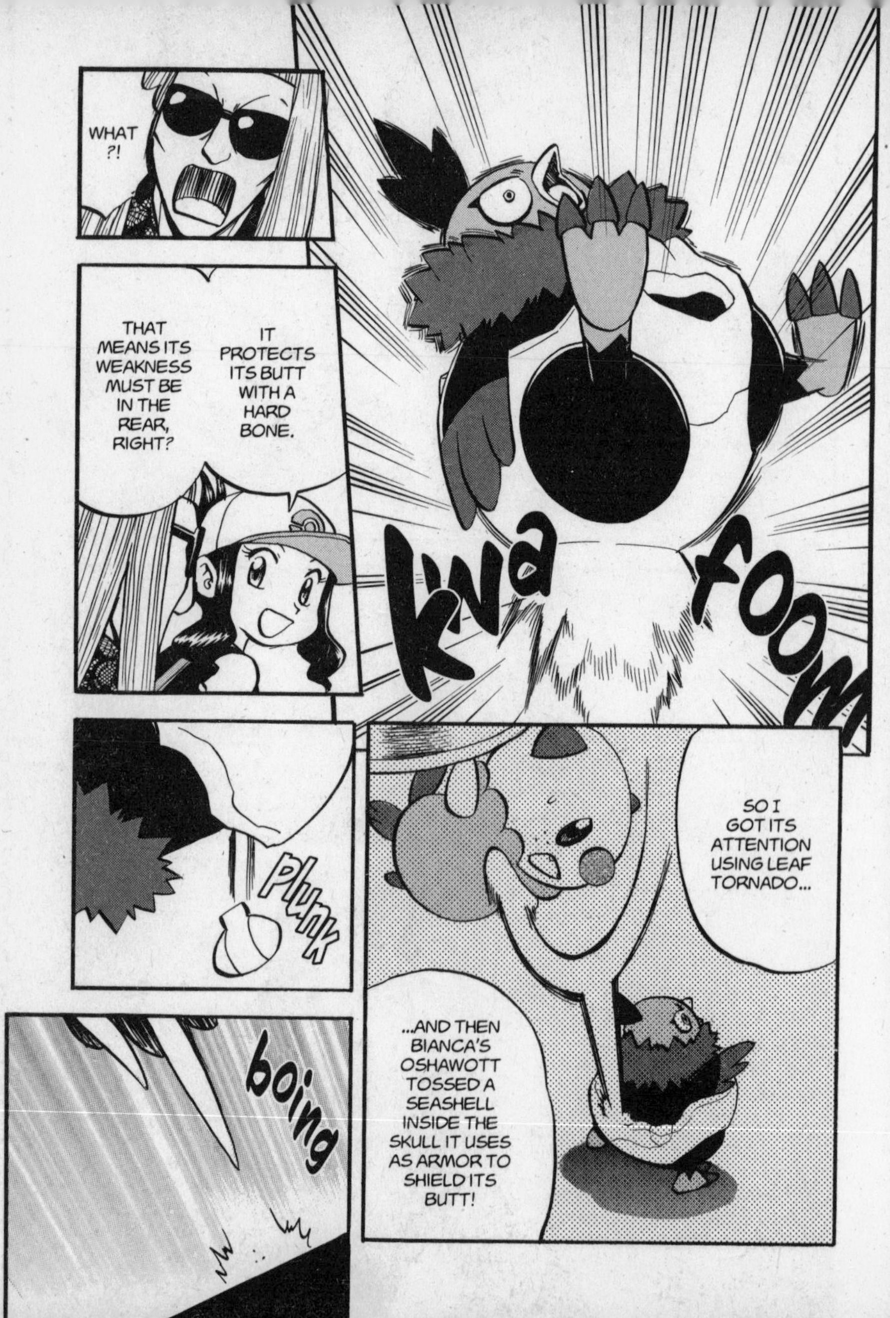
KWA
FOOM
WHAT ?!
IT PROTECTS ITS BUTT WITH A HARD BONE.
THAT MEANS ITS WEAKNESS MUST BE IN THE REAR, RIGHT?
SO I GOT ITS ATTENTION USING LEAF TORNADO...
...AND THEN BIANCA'S OSHAWOTT TOSSED A SEASHELL INSIDE THE SKULL IT USES AS ARMOR TO SHIELD ITS BUTT!
PLUNK
BOING

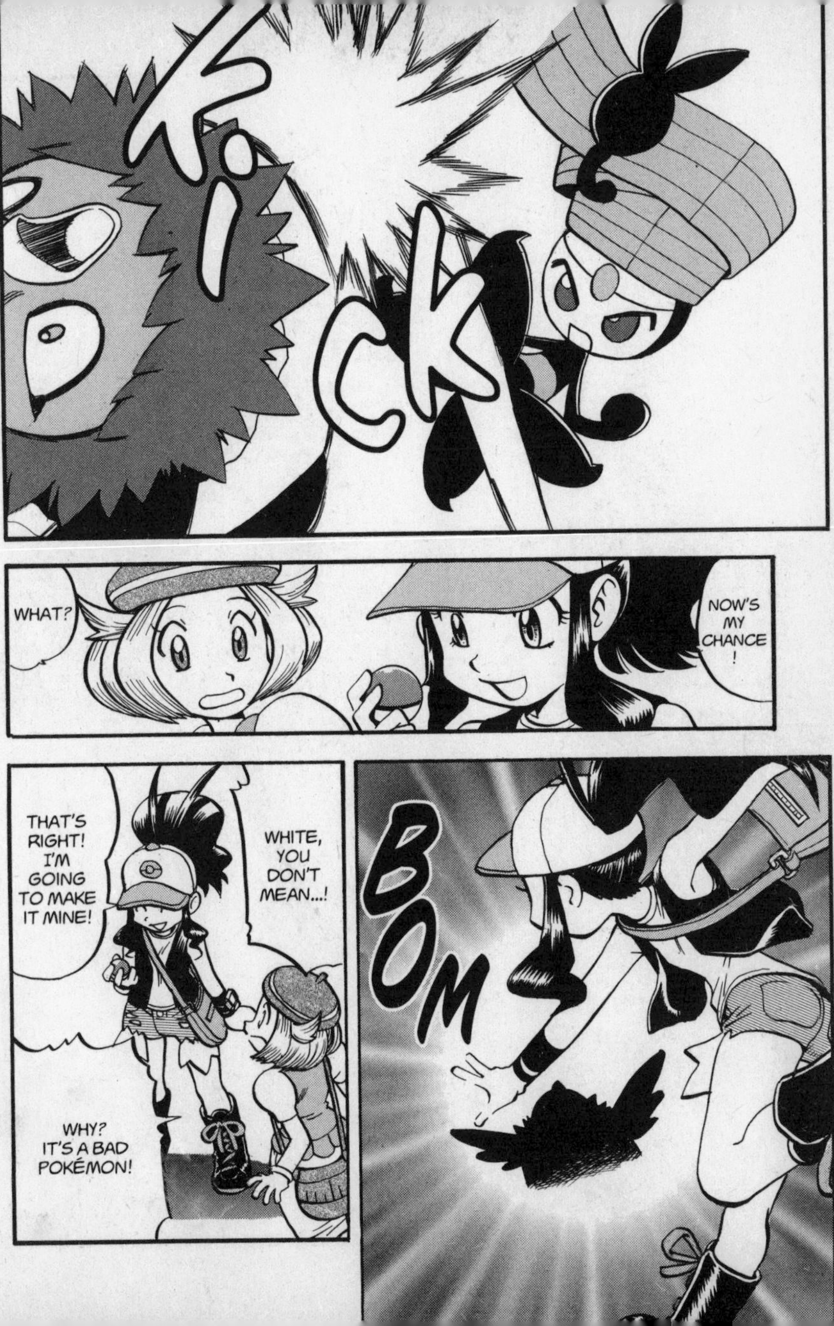
NOW'S MY CHANCE!
WHAT?
BOOM
WHITE, YOU DON'T MEAN...!
THAT'S RIGHT! I'M GOING TO MAKE IT MINE!
WHY? IT'S A BAD POKÉMON!

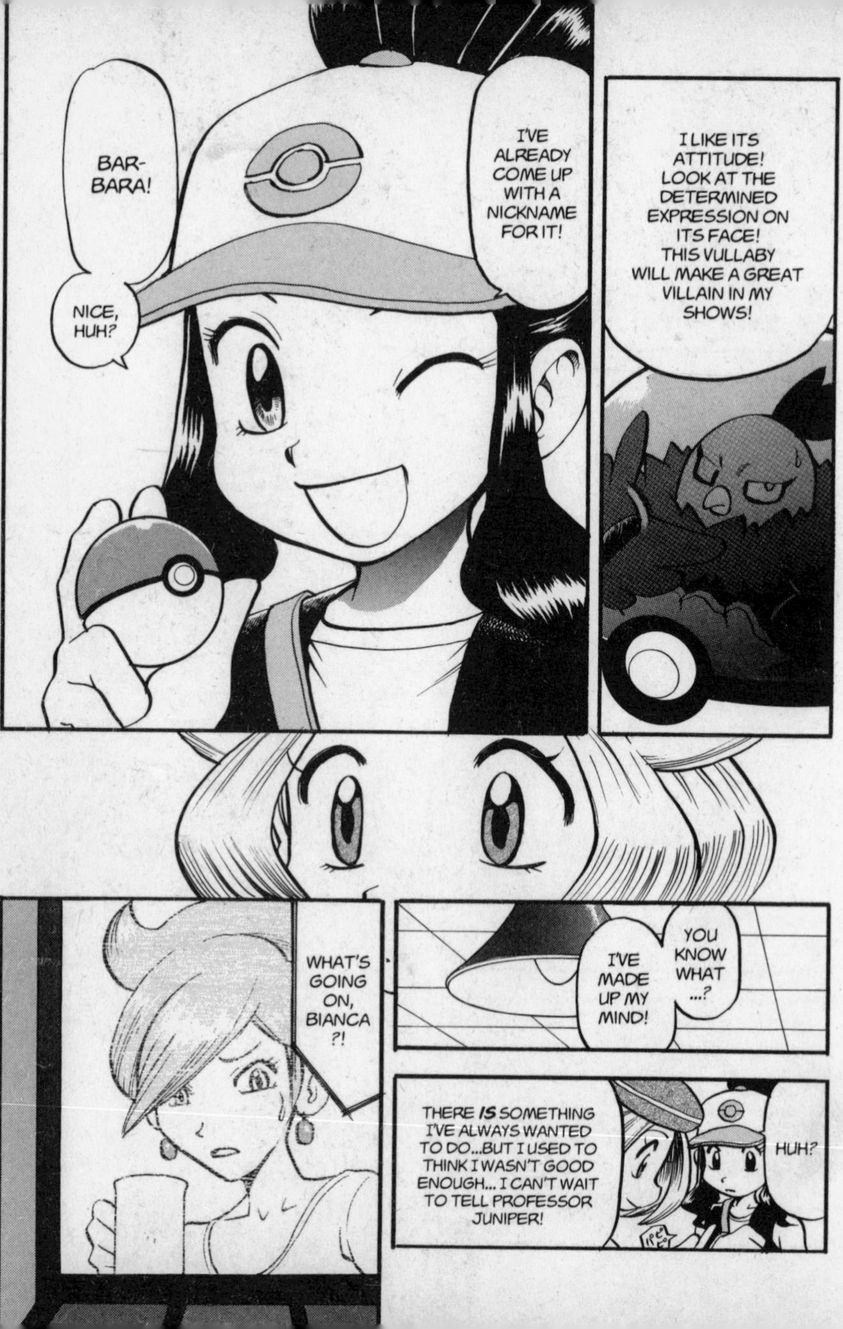
I LIKE ITS ATTITUDE! LOOK AT THE DETERMINED EXPRESSION ON ITS FACE! THIS VULLABY WILL MAKE A GREAT VILLAIN IN MY SHOWS!
I'VE ALREADY COME UP WITH A NICKNAME FOR IT!
BAR-BARA!
NICE, HUH?
YOU KNOW WHAT...?
I'VE MADE UP MY MIND!
HUH?
THERE ***IS*** SOMETHING I'VE ALWAYS WANTED TO DO...BUT I USED TO THINK I WASN'T GOOD ENOUGH... I CAN'T WAIT TO TELL PROFESSOR JUNIPER!
WHAT'S GOING ON, BIANCA?!

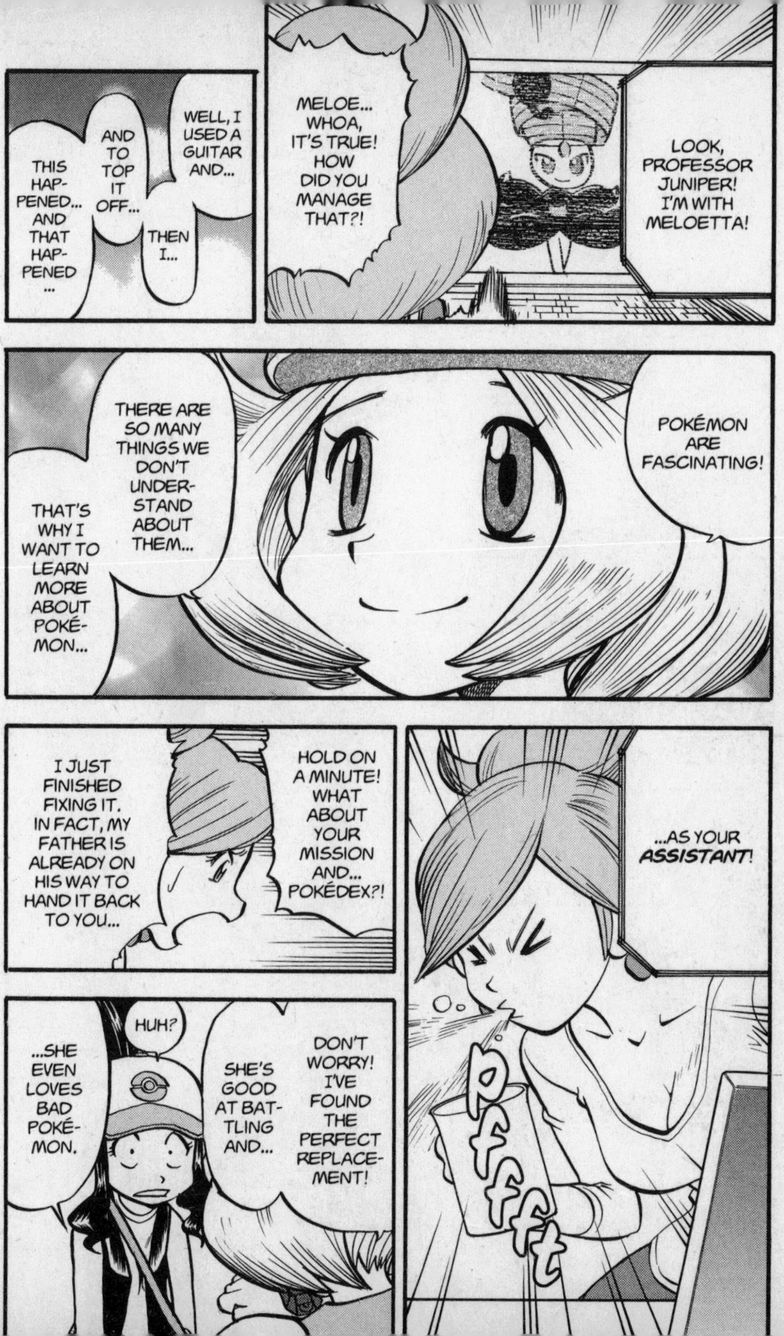
LOOK, PROFESSOR JUNIPER! I'M WITH MELOETTA!
MELOE... WHOA, IT'S TRUE! HOW DID YOU MANAGE THAT?!
WELL, I USED A GUITAR AND...
THEN I...
AND TO TOP IT OFF...
THIS HAPPENED... AND THAT HAPPENED...
POKÉMON ARE FASCINATING!
THERE ARE SO MANY THINGS WE DON'T UNDERSTAND ABOUT THEM...
THAT'S WHY I WANT TO LEARN MORE ABOUT POKÉMON...
...AS YOUR *ASSISTANT*!
pffft
HOLD ON A MINUTE! WHAT ABOUT YOUR MISSION AND... POKÉDEX?!
I JUST FINISHED FIXING IT. IN FACT, MY FATHER IS ALREADY ON HIS WAY TO HAND IT BACK TO YOU...
DON'T WORRY! I'VE FOUND THE PERFECT REPLACEMENT!
SHE'S GOOD AT BATTLING AND...
HUH?
...SHE EVEN LOVES BAD POKÉMON.

I WANT **HER** TO HAVE MY POKÉDEX!!

MEET WHITE!

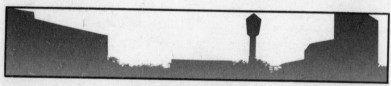

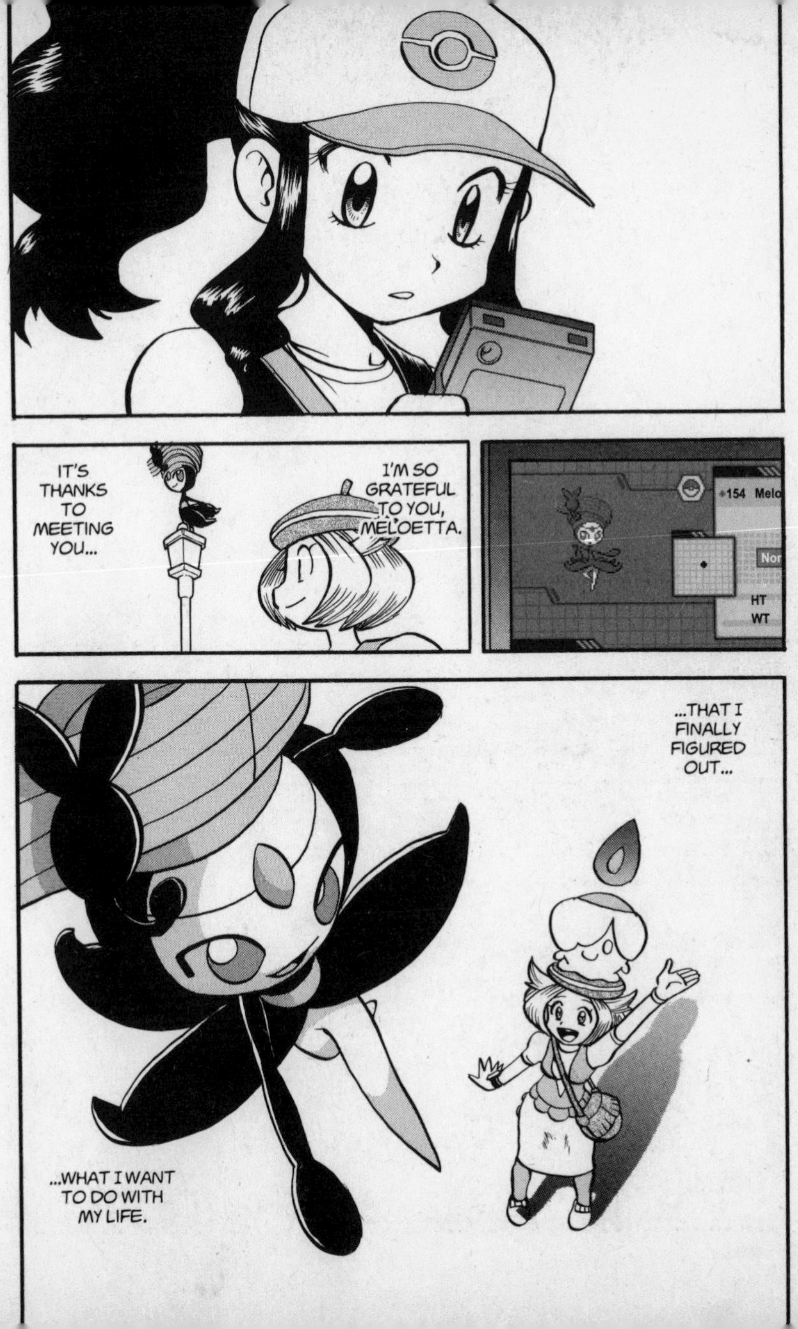
154 Melo
Nor
HT
WT
I'M SO GRATEFUL TO YOU, MELOETTA.
IT'S THANKS TO MEETING YOU...
...THAT I FINALLY FIGURED OUT...
...WHAT I WANT TO DO WITH MY LIFE.

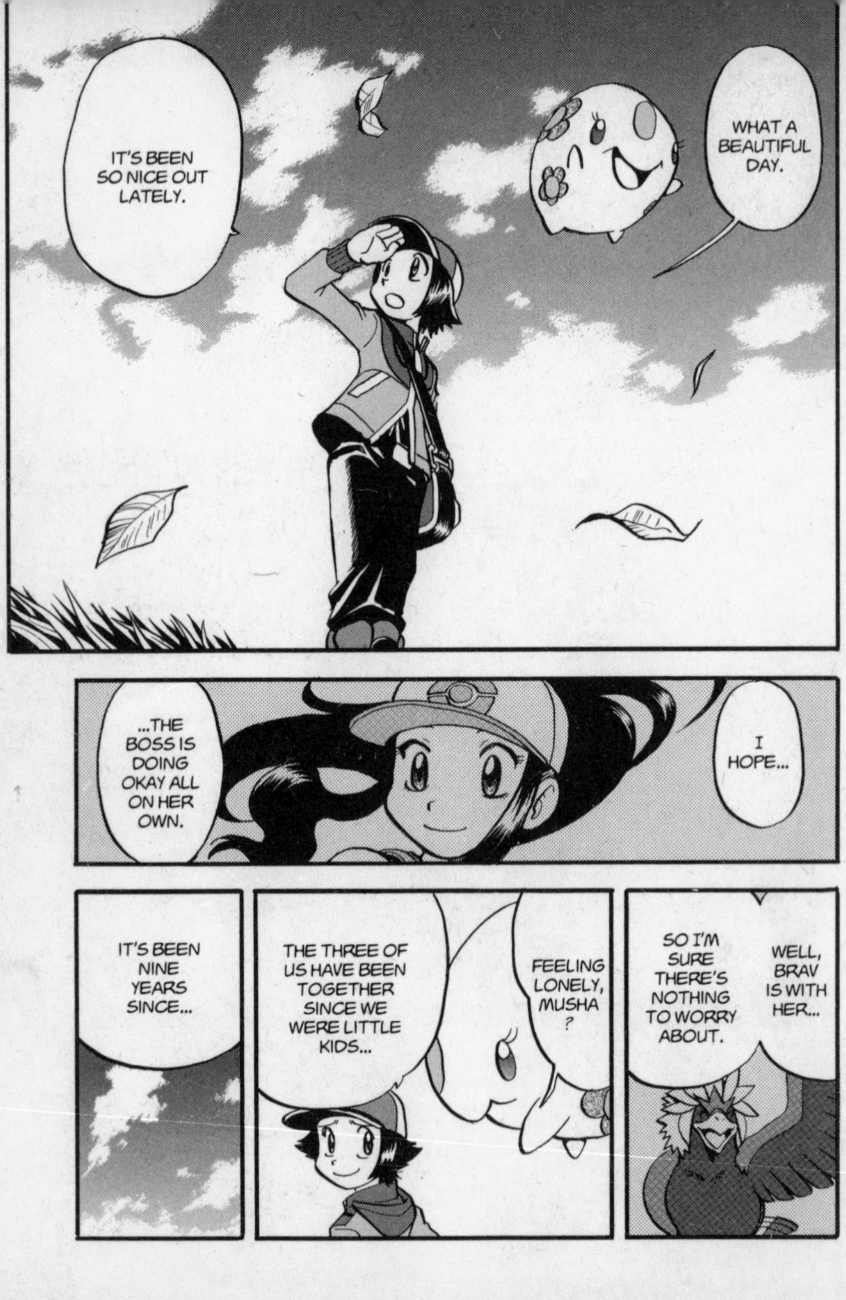
WHAT A BEAUTIFUL DAY.
IT'S BEEN SO NICE OUT LATELY.
I HOPE...
...THE BOSS IS DOING OKAY ALL ON HER OWN.
WELL, BRAV IS WITH HER...
SO I'M SURE THERE'S NOTHING TO WORRY ABOUT.
FEELING LONELY, MUSHA?
THE THREE OF US HAVE BEEN TOGETHER SINCE WE WERE LITTLE KIDS...
IT'S BEEN NINE YEARS SINCE...

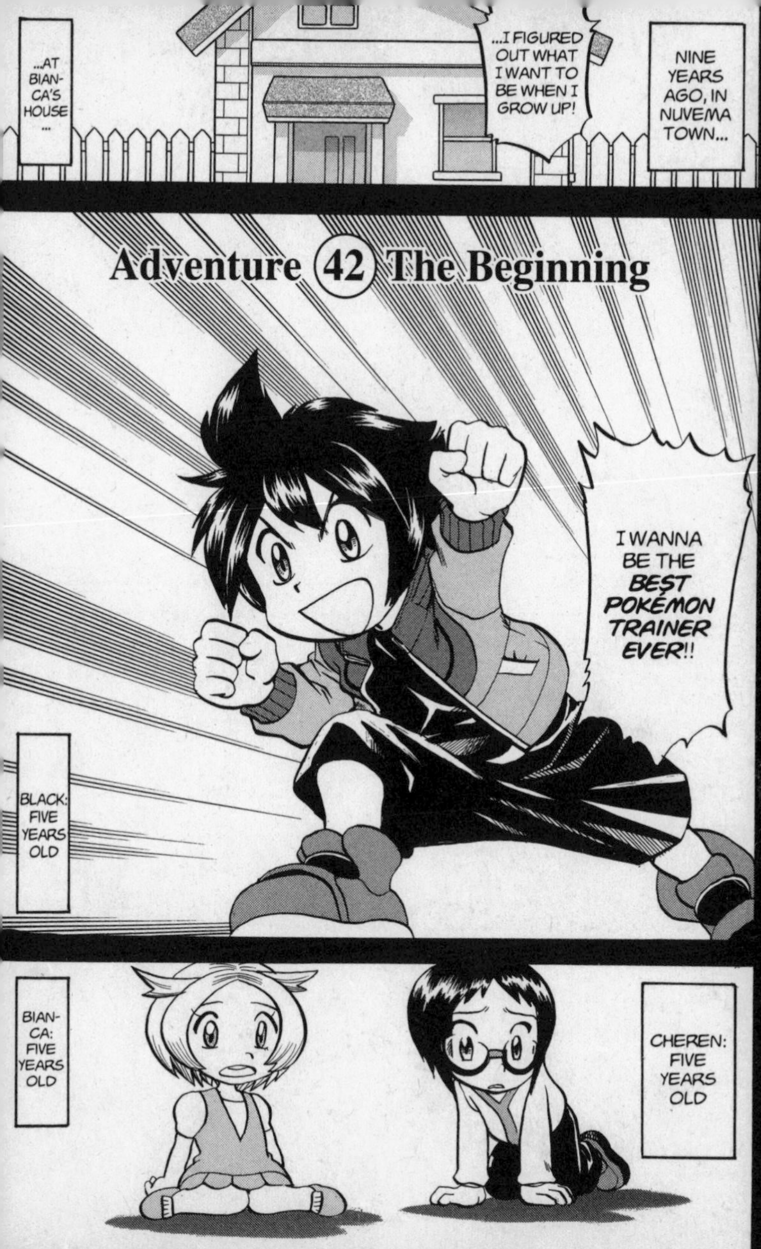
NINE YEARS AGO, IN NUVEMA TOWN...
...I FIGURED OUT WHAT I WANT TO BE WHEN I GROW UP!
...AT BIANCA'S HOUSE...
Adventure 42 The Beginning
I WANNA BE THE BEST POKÉMON TRAINER EVER!!
BLACK: FIVE YEARS OLD
CHEREN: FIVE YEARS OLD
BIANCA: FIVE YEARS OLD

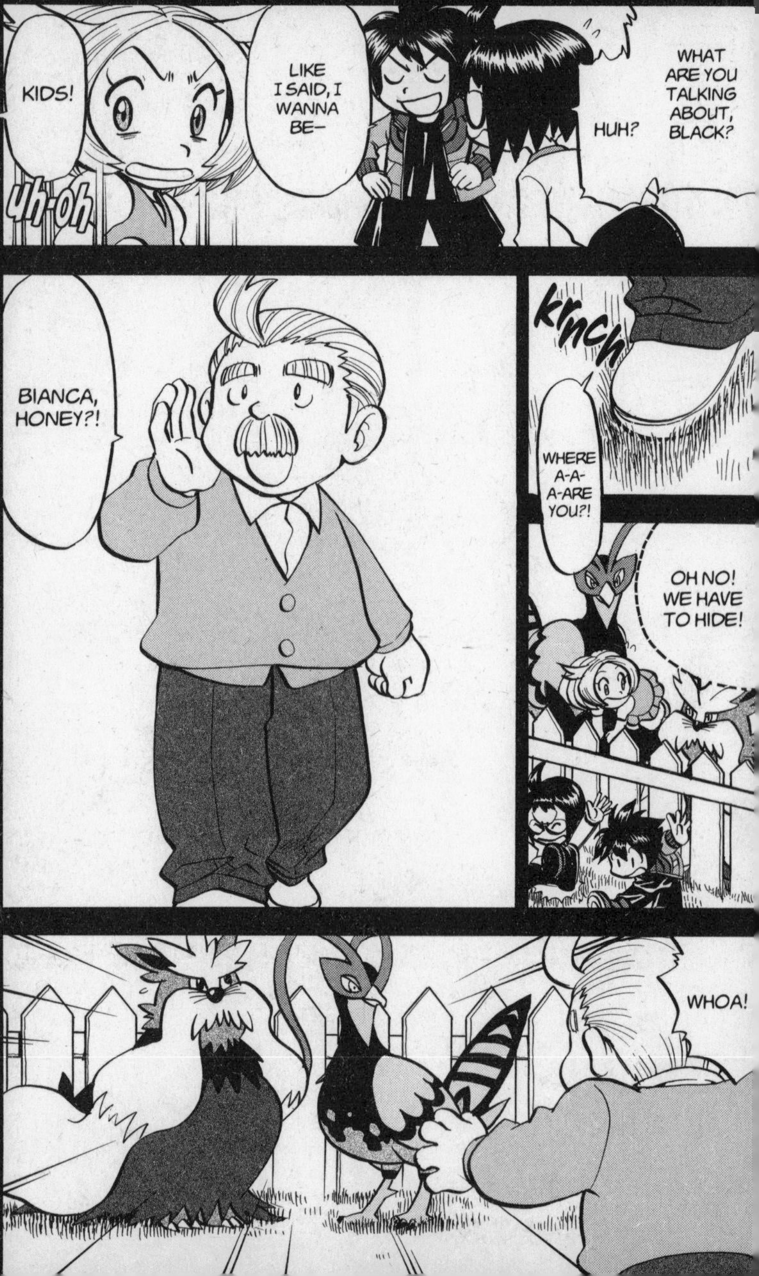
WHAT ARE YOU TALKING ABOUT, BLACK?
HUH?
LIKE I SAID, I WANNA BE–
KIDS!
uh-oh
krnch
WHERE A-A-A-ARE YOU?!
OH NO! WE HAVE TO HIDE!
BIANCA, HONEY?!
WHOA!

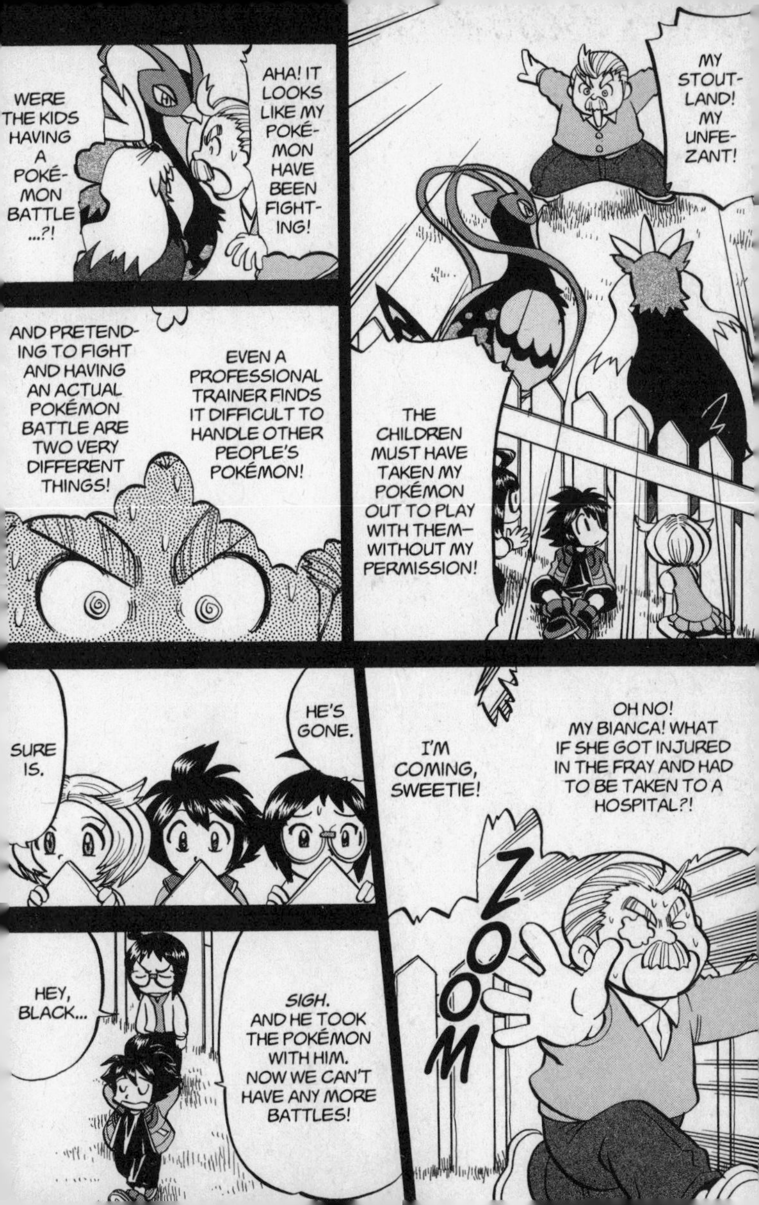
MY STOUTLAND! MY UNFEZANT!
THE CHILDREN MUST HAVE TAKEN MY POKÉMON OUT TO PLAY WITH THEM— WITHOUT MY PERMISSION!
AHA! IT LOOKS LIKE MY POKÉMON HAVE BEEN FIGHTING!
WERE THE KIDS HAVING A POKÉMON BATTLE ...?!
EVEN A PROFESSIONAL TRAINER FINDS IT DIFFICULT TO HANDLE OTHER PEOPLE'S POKÉMON!
AND PRETENDING TO FIGHT AND HAVING AN ACTUAL POKÉMON BATTLE ARE TWO VERY DIFFERENT THINGS!
OH NO! MY BIANCA! WHAT IF SHE GOT INJURED IN THE FRAY AND HAD TO BE TAKEN TO A HOSPITAL?!
I'M COMING, SWEETIE!
ZOOOM
HE'S GONE.
SURE IS.
SIGH. AND HE TOOK THE POKÉMON WITH HIM. NOW WE CAN'T HAVE ANY MORE BATTLES!
HEY, BLACK...

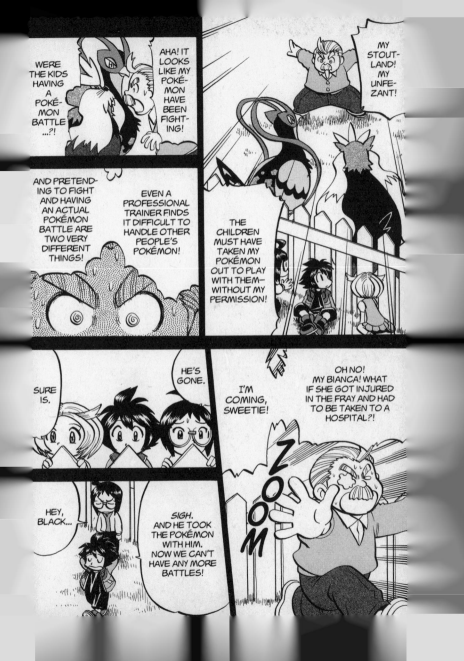

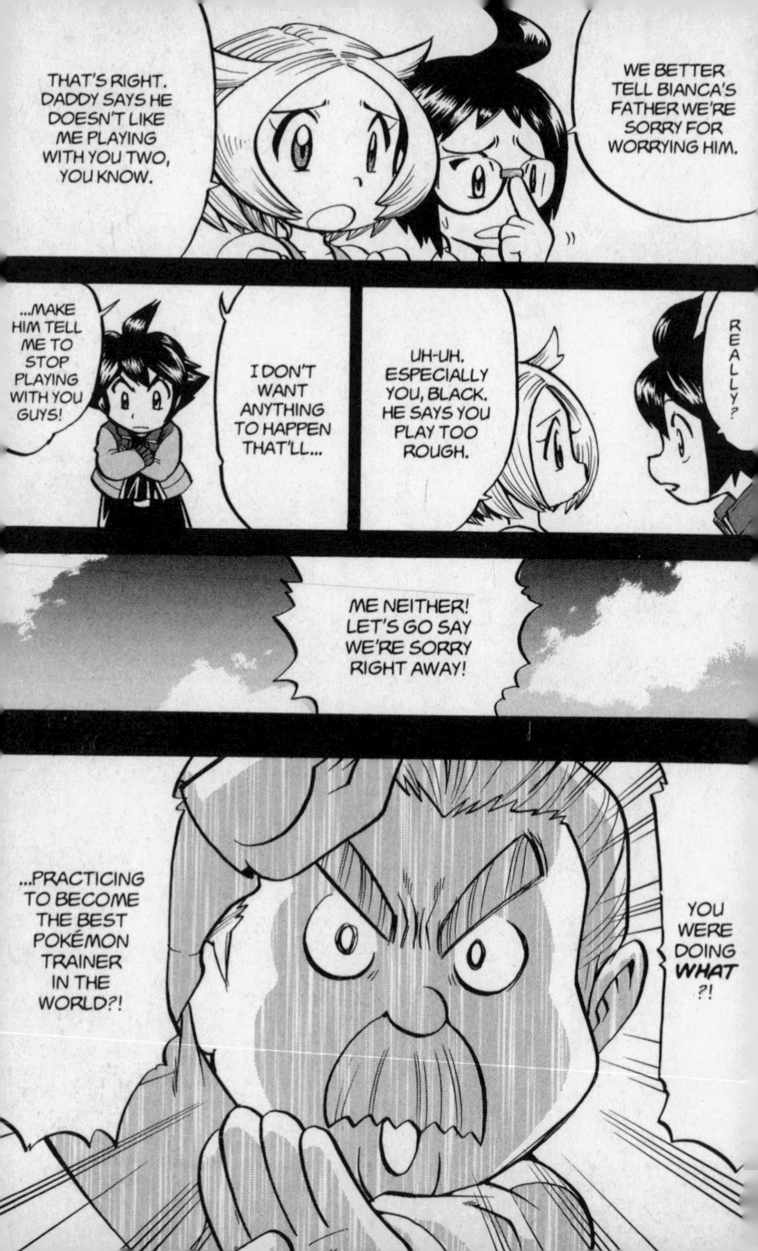
WE BETTER TELL BIANCA'S FATHER WE'RE SORRY FOR WORRYING HIM.
THAT'S RIGHT. DADDY SAYS HE DOESN'T LIKE ME PLAYING WITH YOU TWO, YOU KNOW.
REALLY?
UH-UH. ESPECIALLY YOU, BLACK. HE SAYS YOU PLAY TOO ROUGH.
I DON'T WANT ANYTHING TO HAPPEN THAT'LL...
...MAKE HIM TELL ME TO STOP PLAYING WITH YOU GUYS!
ME NEITHER! LET'S GO SAY WE'RE SORRY RIGHT AWAY!
YOU WERE DOING ***WHAT***?!
...PRACTICING TO BECOME THE BEST POKÉMON TRAINER IN THE WORLD?!

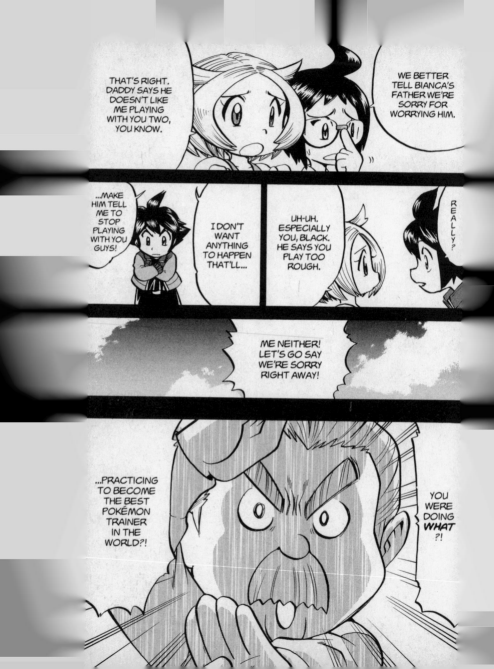

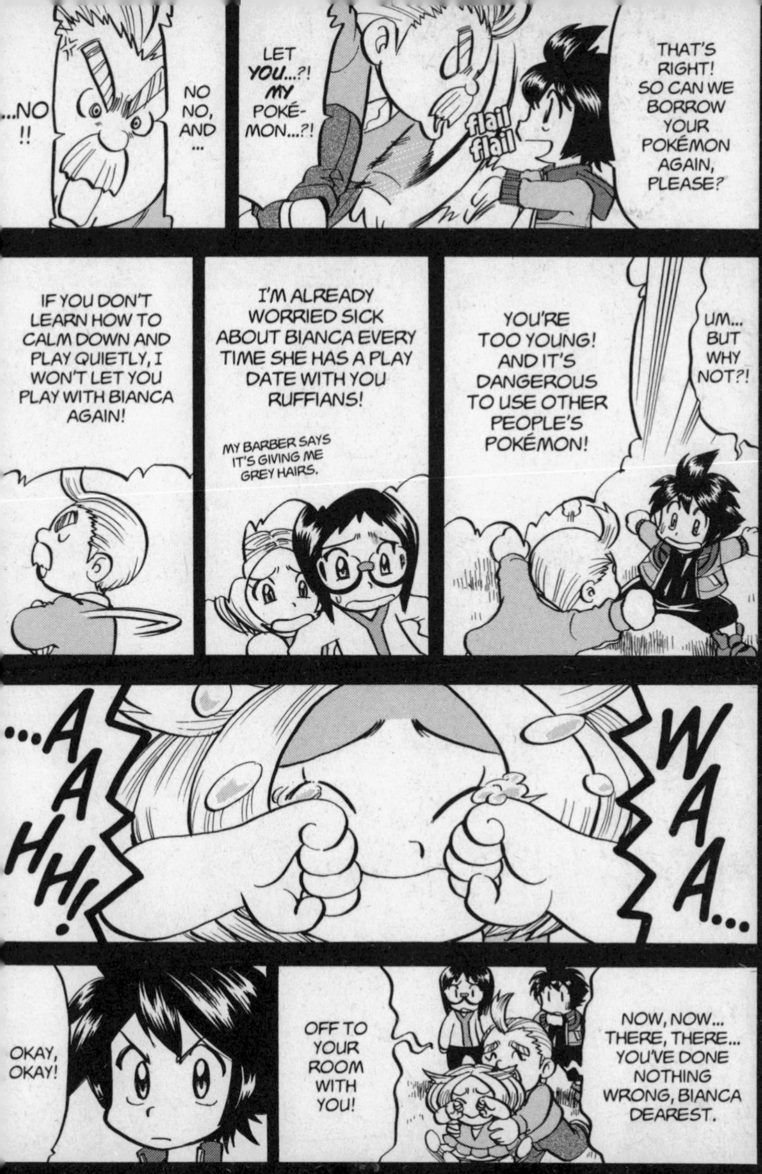
THAT'S RIGHT! SO CAN WE BORROW YOUR POKÉMON AGAIN, PLEASE?
flail flail
LET YOU...?! MY POKÉ-MON...?!
NO NO, AND ...
...NO !!
UM... BUT WHY NOT?!
YOU'RE TOO YOUNG! AND IT'S DANGEROUS TO USE OTHER PEOPLE'S POKÉMON!
I'M ALREADY WORRIED SICK ABOUT BIANCA EVERY TIME SHE HAS A PLAY DATE WITH YOU RUFFIANS!
MY BARBER SAYS IT'S GIVING ME GREY HAIRS.
IF YOU DON'T LEARN HOW TO CALM DOWN AND PLAY QUIETLY, I WON'T LET YOU PLAY WITH BIANCA AGAIN!
WAAA...
...AAAHH!!
NOW, NOW... THERE, THERE... YOU'VE DONE NOTHING WRONG, BIANCA DEAREST.
OFF TO YOUR ROOM WITH YOU!
OKAY, OKAY!

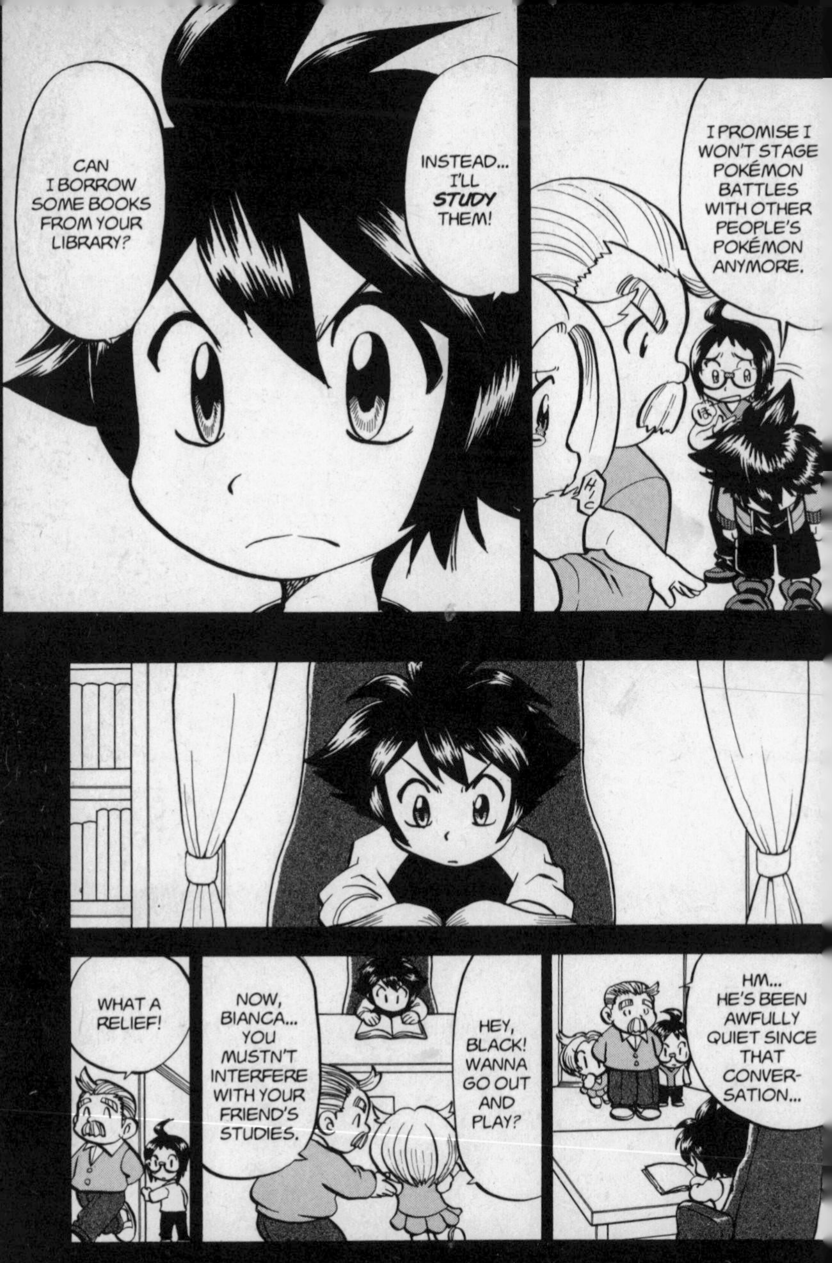
I PROMISE I WON'T STAGE POKÉMON BATTLES WITH OTHER PEOPLE'S POKÉMON ANYMORE.
INSTEAD... I'LL **STUDY** THEM!
CAN I BORROW SOME BOOKS FROM YOUR LIBRARY?
HM... HE'S BEEN AWFULLY QUIET SINCE THAT CONVER-SATION...
HEY, BLACK! WANNA GO OUT AND PLAY?
NOW, BIANCA... YOU MUSTN'T INTERFERE WITH YOUR FRIEND'S STUDIES.
WHAT A RELIEF!

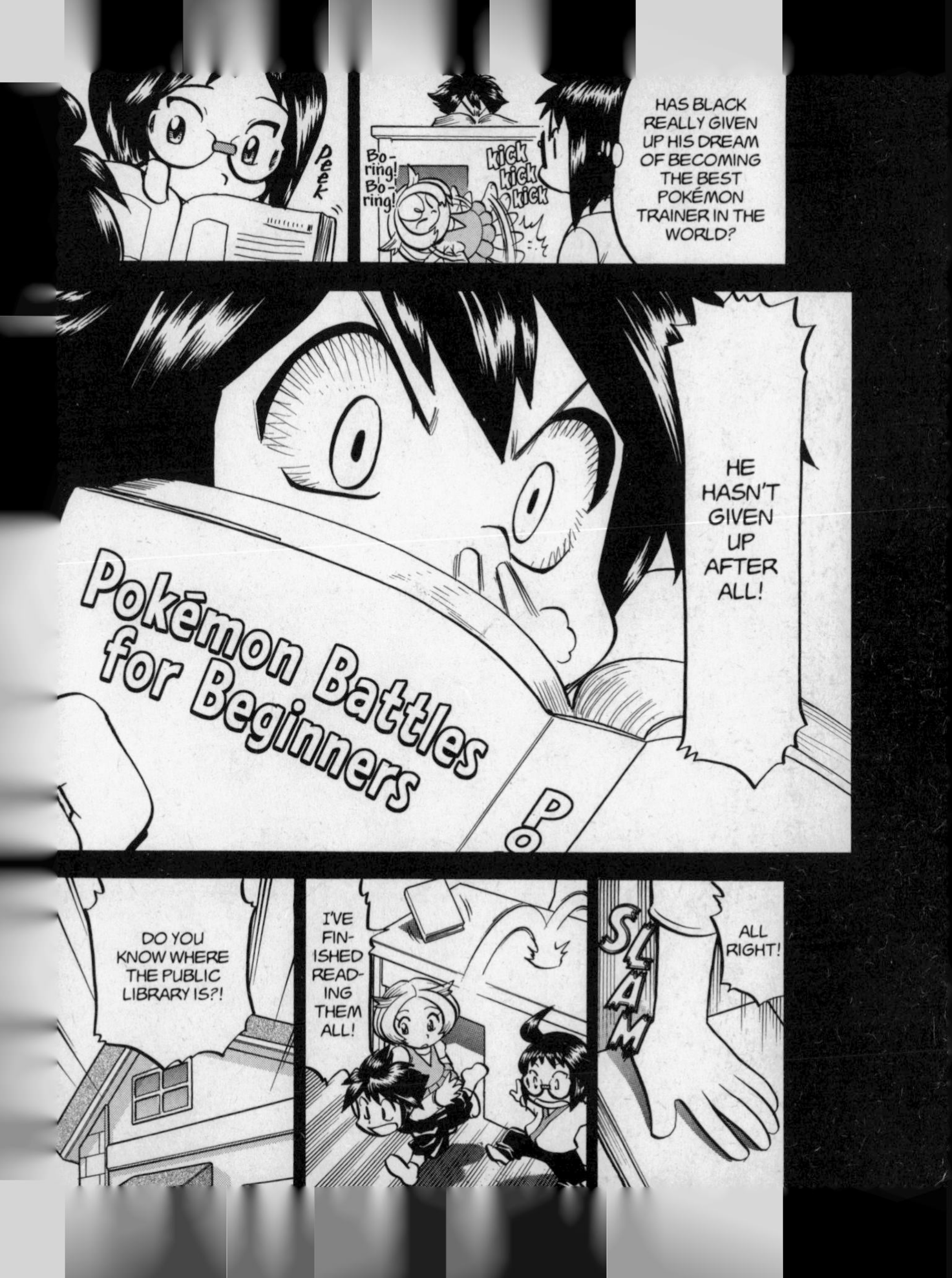
HAS BLACK REALLY GIVEN UP HIS DREAM OF BECOMING THE BEST POKÉMON TRAINER IN THE WORLD?
kick kick kick
Bo-ring! Bo-ring!
Peek
HE HASN'T GIVEN UP AFTER ALL!
Pokēmon Battles for Beginners
Po
ALL RIGHT!
SLAM
I'VE FIN-ISHED READ-ING THEM ALL!
DO YOU KNOW WHERE THE PUBLIC LIBRARY IS?!

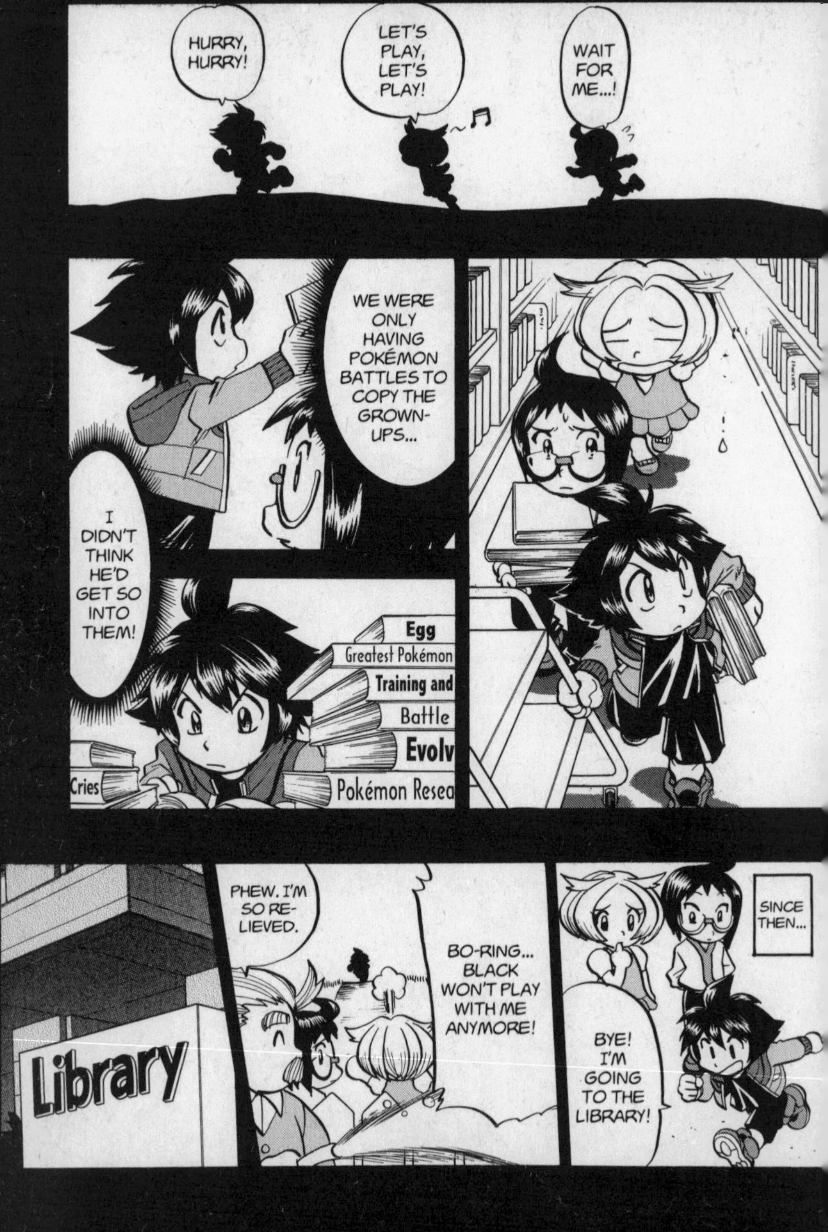
WAIT FOR ME...!
LET'S PLAY, LET'S PLAY!
HURRY, HURRY!
WE WERE ONLY HAVING POKÉMON BATTLES TO COPY THE GROWN-UPS...
I DIDN'T THINK HE'D GET SO INTO THEM!
Egg
Greatest Pokémon
Training and
Battle
Evolv
Cries
Pokémon Resea
SINCE THEN...
BYE! I'M GOING TO THE LIBRARY!
BO-RING... BLACK WON'T PLAY WITH ME ANYMORE!
PHEW. I'M SO RE-LIEVED.
Library

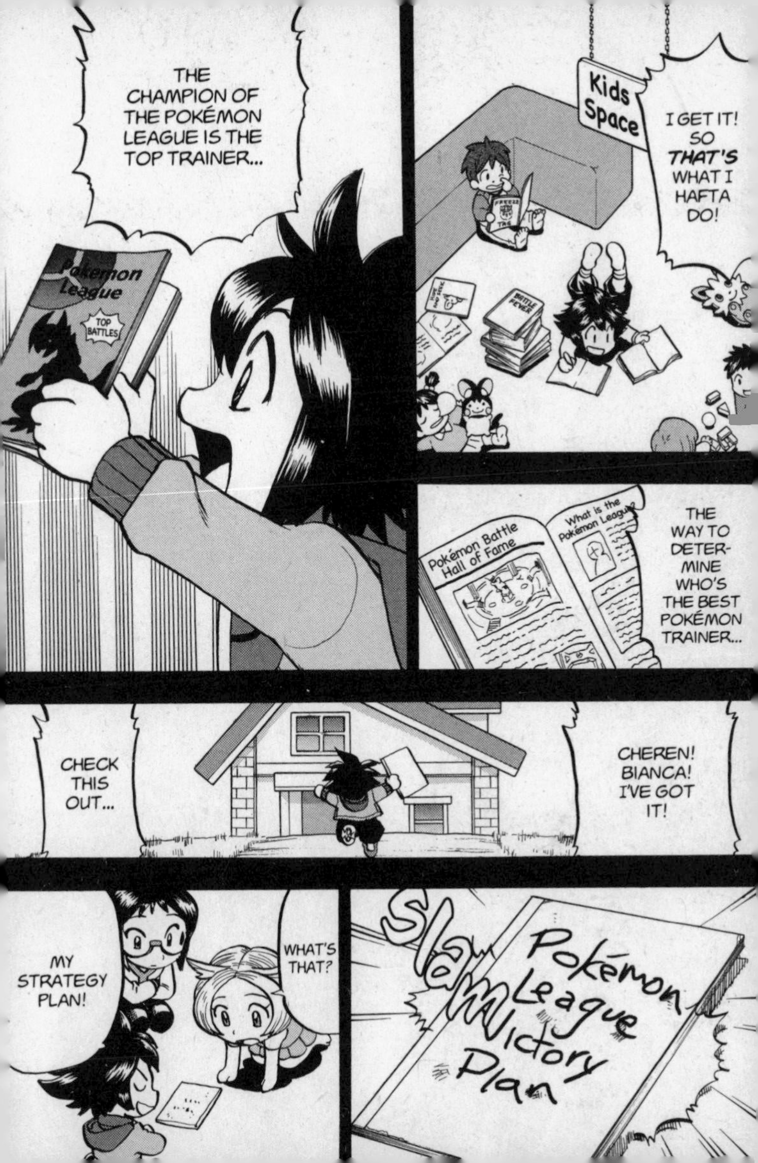
Kids Space
I GET IT! SO THAT'S WHAT I HAFTA DO!
BATTLE FEVER
What is the Pokémon League?
Pokémon Battle Hall of Fame
THE WAY TO DETERMINE WHO'S THE BEST POKÉMON TRAINER...
THE CHAMPION OF THE POKÉMON LEAGUE IS THE TOP TRAINER...
Pokémon League
TOP BATTLES
CHEREN! BIANCA! I'VE GOT IT!
CHECK THIS OUT...
SLAM
Pokémon League Victory Plan
WHAT'S THAT?
MY STRATEGY PLAN!

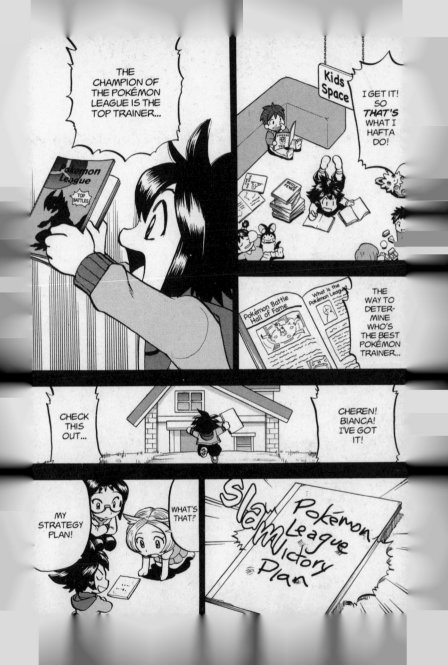

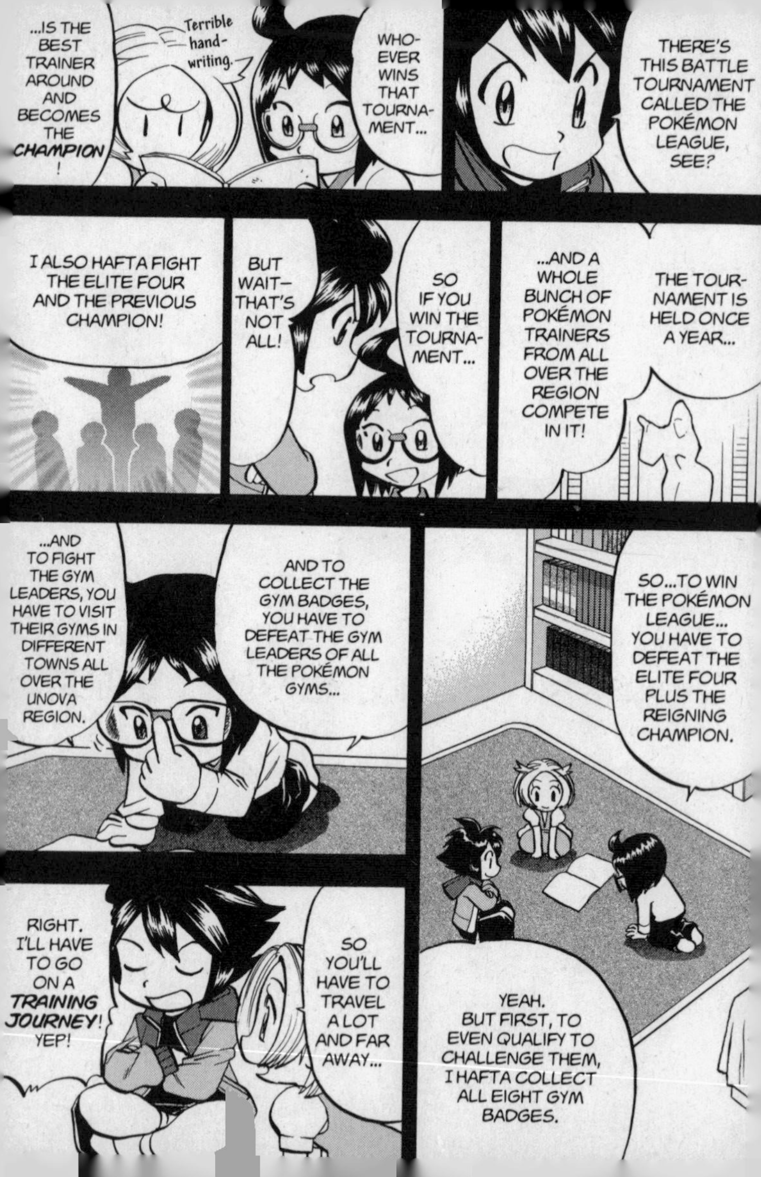
THERE'S THIS BATTLE TOURNAMENT CALLED THE POKÉMON LEAGUE, SEE?
WHO-EVER WINS THAT TOURNA-MENT...
Terrible hand-writing.
...IS THE BEST TRAINER AROUND AND BECOMES THE CHAMPION!
THE TOUR-NAMENT IS HELD ONCE A YEAR...
...AND A WHOLE BUNCH OF POKÉMON TRAINERS FROM ALL OVER THE REGION COMPETE IN IT!
SO IF YOU WIN THE TOURNA-MENT...
BUT WAIT—THAT'S NOT ALL!
I ALSO HAFTA FIGHT THE ELITE FOUR AND THE PREVIOUS CHAMPION!
SO...TO WIN THE POKÉMON LEAGUE... YOU HAVE TO DEFEAT THE ELITE FOUR PLUS THE REIGNING CHAMPION.
YEAH. BUT FIRST, TO EVEN QUALIFY TO CHALLENGE THEM, I HAFTA COLLECT ALL EIGHT GYM BADGES.
AND TO COLLECT THE GYM BADGES, YOU HAVE TO DEFEAT THE GYM LEADERS OF ALL THE POKÉMON GYMS...
...AND TO FIGHT THE GYM LEADERS, YOU HAVE TO VISIT THEIR GYMS IN DIFFERENT TOWNS ALL OVER THE UNOVA REGION.
SO YOU'LL HAVE TO TRAVEL A LOT AND FAR AWAY...
RIGHT. I'LL HAVE TO GO ON A TRAINING JOURNEY! YEP!

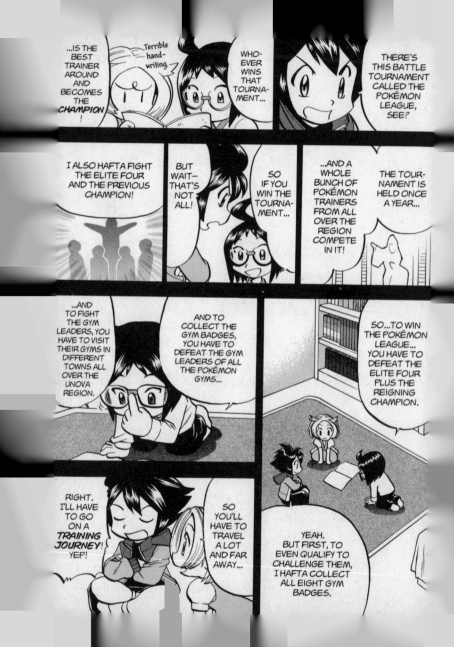

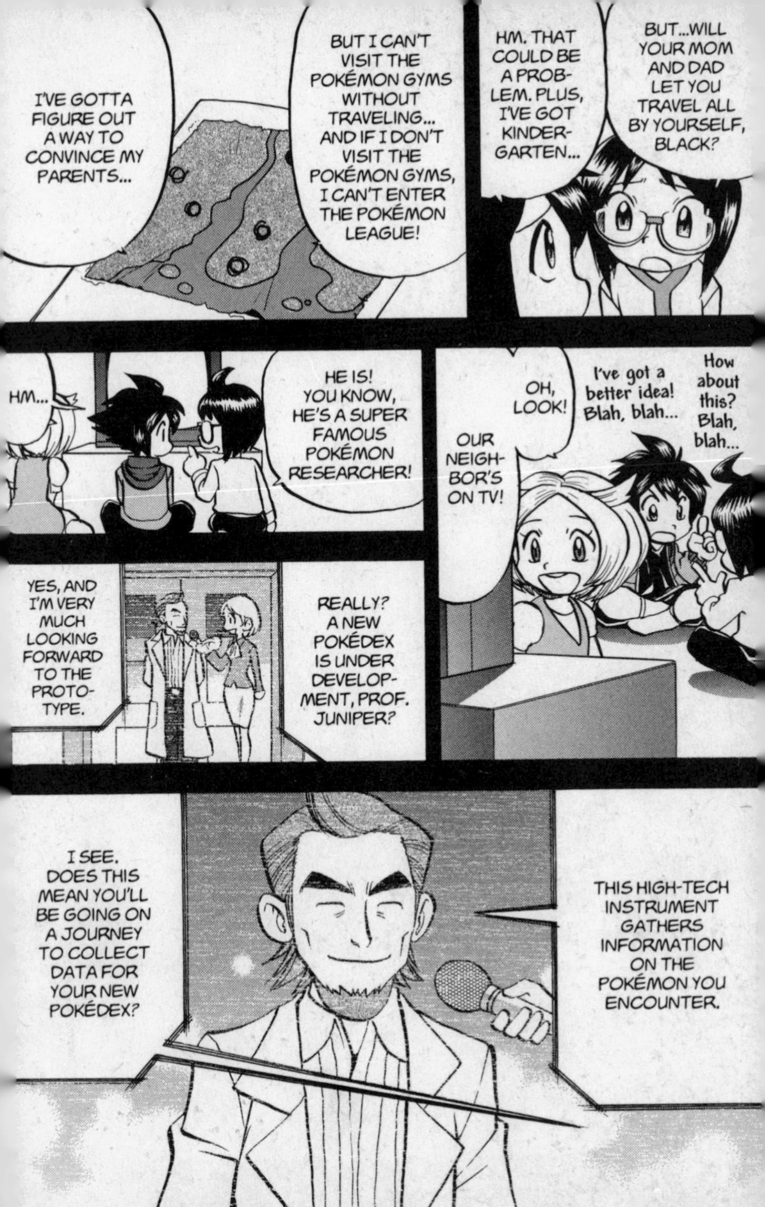
BUT...WILL YOUR MOM AND DAD LET YOU TRAVEL ALL BY YOURSELF, BLACK?
HM. THAT COULD BE A PROB-LEM. PLUS, I'VE GOT KINDER-GARTEN...
BUT I CAN'T VISIT THE POKÉMON GYMS WITHOUT TRAVELING... AND IF I DON'T VISIT THE POKÉMON GYMS, I CAN'T ENTER THE POKÉMON LEAGUE!
I'VE GOTTA FIGURE OUT A WAY TO CONVINCE MY PARENTS...
How about this? Blah, blah...
I've got a better idea! Blah, blah...
OH, LOOK!
OUR NEIGH-BOR'S ON TV!
HE IS! YOU KNOW, HE'S A SUPER FAMOUS POKÉMON RESEARCHER!
HM...
REALLY? A NEW POKÉDEX IS UNDER DEVELOP-MENT, PROF. JUNIPER?
YES, AND I'M VERY MUCH LOOKING FORWARD TO THE PROTO-TYPE.
THIS HIGH-TECH INSTRUMENT GATHERS INFORMATION ON THE POKÉMON YOU ENCOUNTER.
I SEE. DOES THIS MEAN YOU'LL BE GOING ON A JOURNEY TO COLLECT DATA FOR YOUR NEW POKÉDEX?

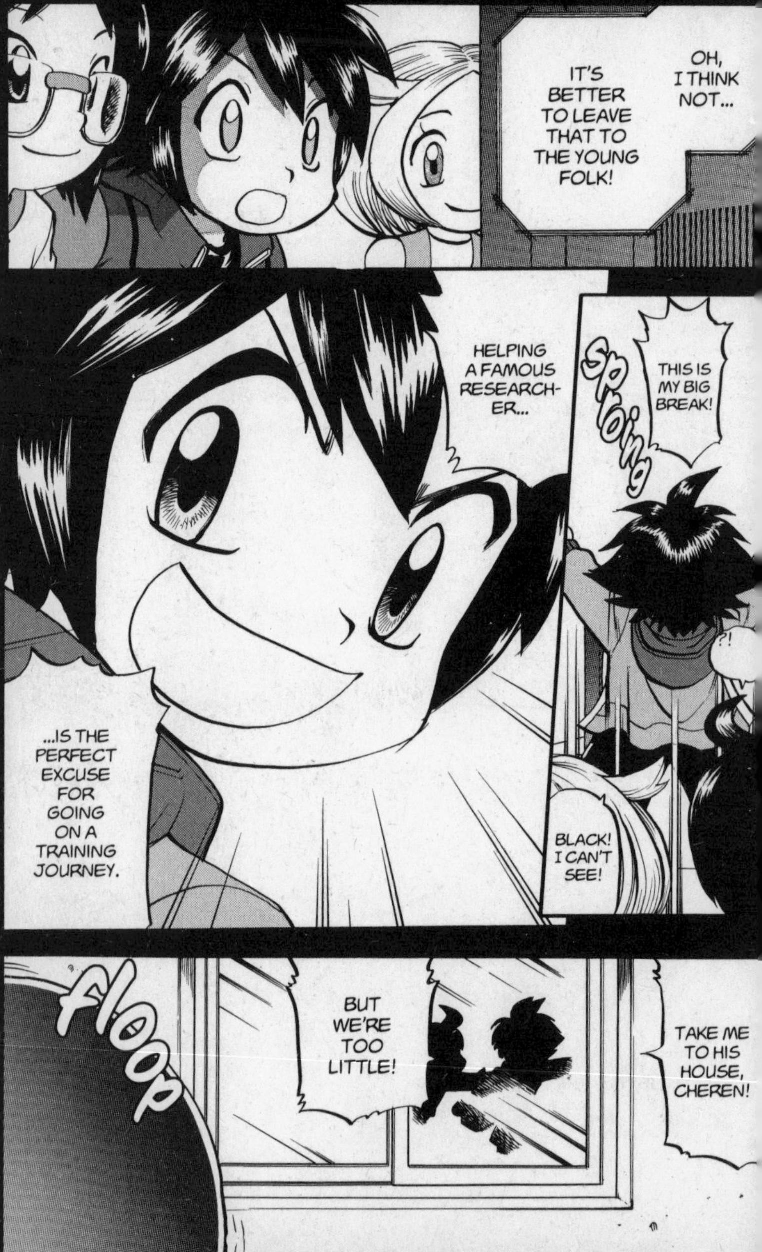
OH, I THINK NOT...
IT'S BETTER TO LEAVE THAT TO THE YOUNG FOLK!
THIS IS MY BIG BREAK!
Spoing
?!
BLACK! I CAN'T SEE!
HELPING A FAMOUS RESEARCHER...
...IS THE PERFECT EXCUSE FOR GOING ON A TRAINING JOURNEY.
TAKE ME TO HIS HOUSE, CHEREN!
BUT WE'RE TOO LITTLE!
floop

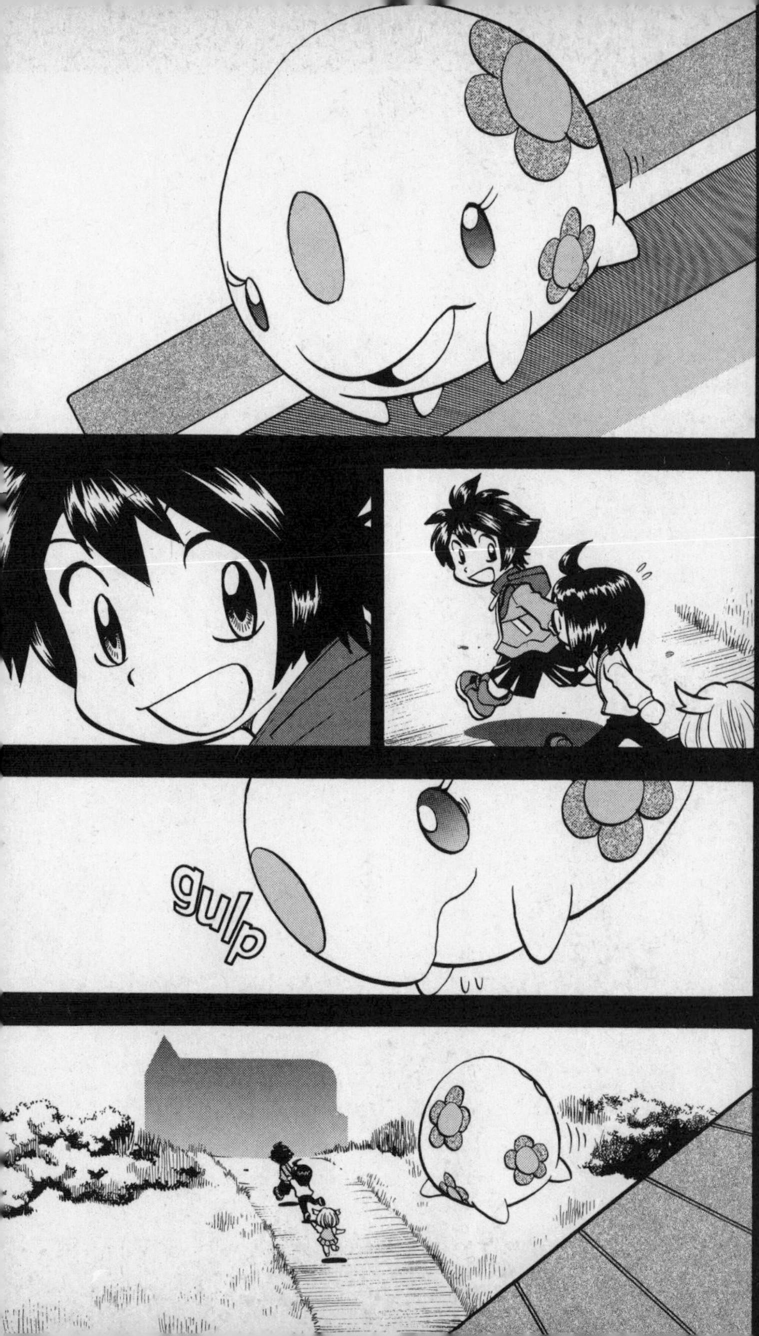
gulp

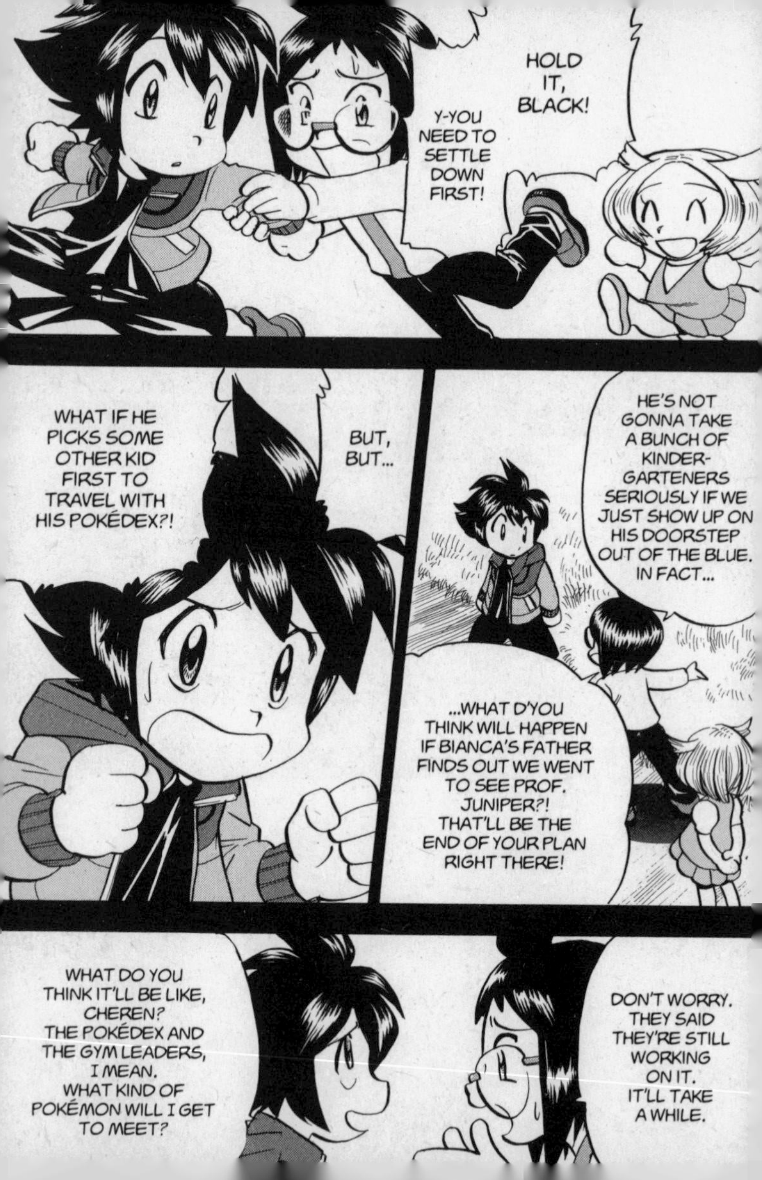
HOLD IT, BLACK!
Y-YOU NEED TO SETTLE DOWN FIRST!
HE'S NOT GONNA TAKE A BUNCH OF KINDER-GARTENERS SERIOUSLY IF WE JUST SHOW UP ON HIS DOORSTEP OUT OF THE BLUE. IN FACT...
...WHAT D'YOU THINK WILL HAPPEN IF BIANCA'S FATHER FINDS OUT WE WENT TO SEE PROF. JUNIPER?! THAT'LL BE THE END OF YOUR PLAN RIGHT THERE!
BUT, BUT...
WHAT IF HE PICKS SOME OTHER KID FIRST TO TRAVEL WITH HIS POKÉDEX?!
DON'T WORRY. THEY SAID THEY'RE STILL WORKING ON IT. IT'LL TAKE A WHILE.
WHAT DO YOU THINK IT'LL BE LIKE, CHEREN? THE POKÉDEX AND THE GYM LEADERS, I MEAN. WHAT KIND OF POKÉMON WILL I GET TO MEET?

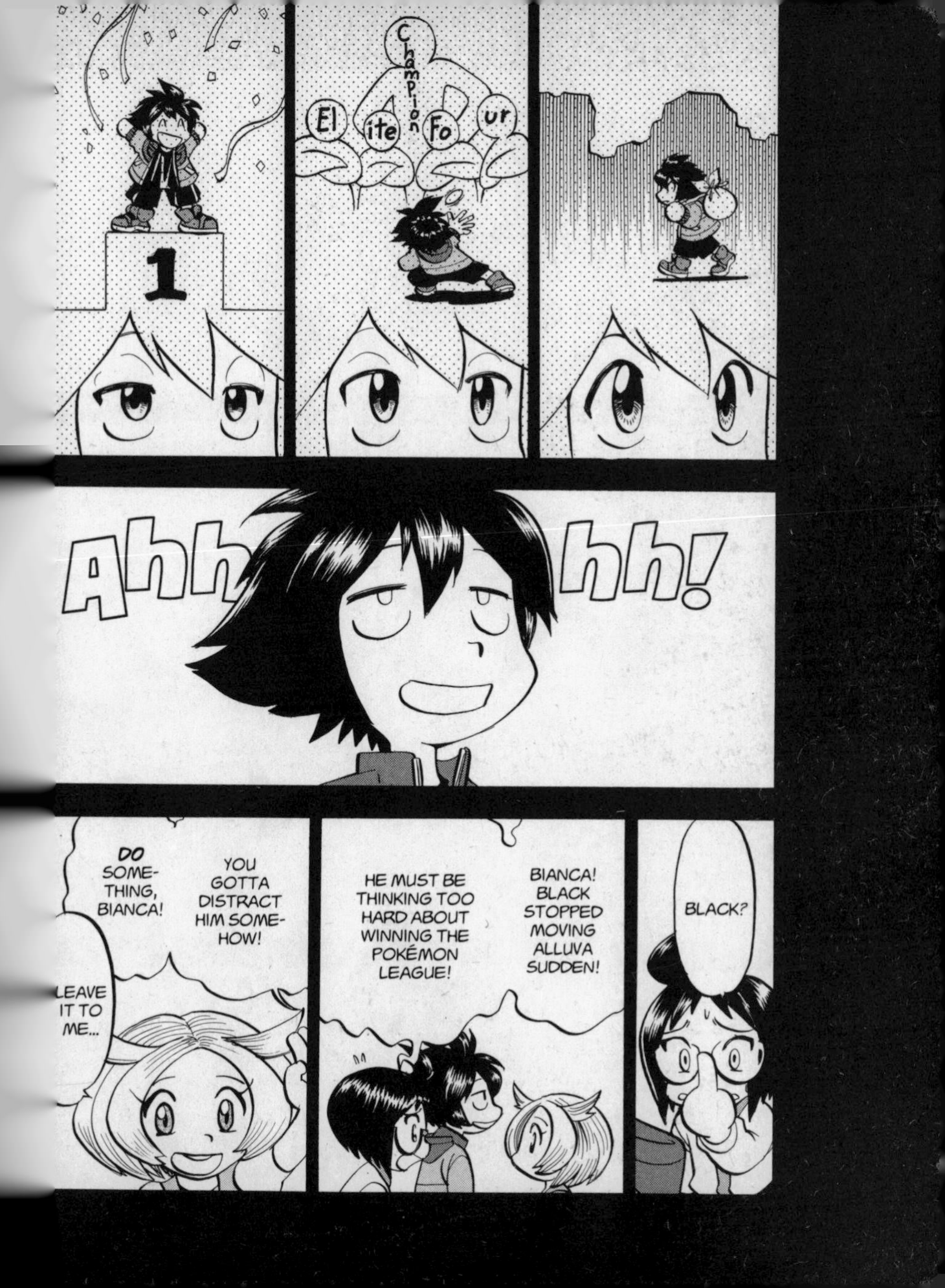
Champion
Elite Four
Ahhhh!
BLACK?
BIANCA! BLACK STOPPED MOVING ALLUVA SUDDEN!
HE MUST BE THINKING TOO HARD ABOUT WINNING THE POKÉMON LEAGUE!
YOU GOTTA DISTRACT HIM SOME-HOW!
DO SOME-THING, BIANCA!
LEAVE IT TO ME...

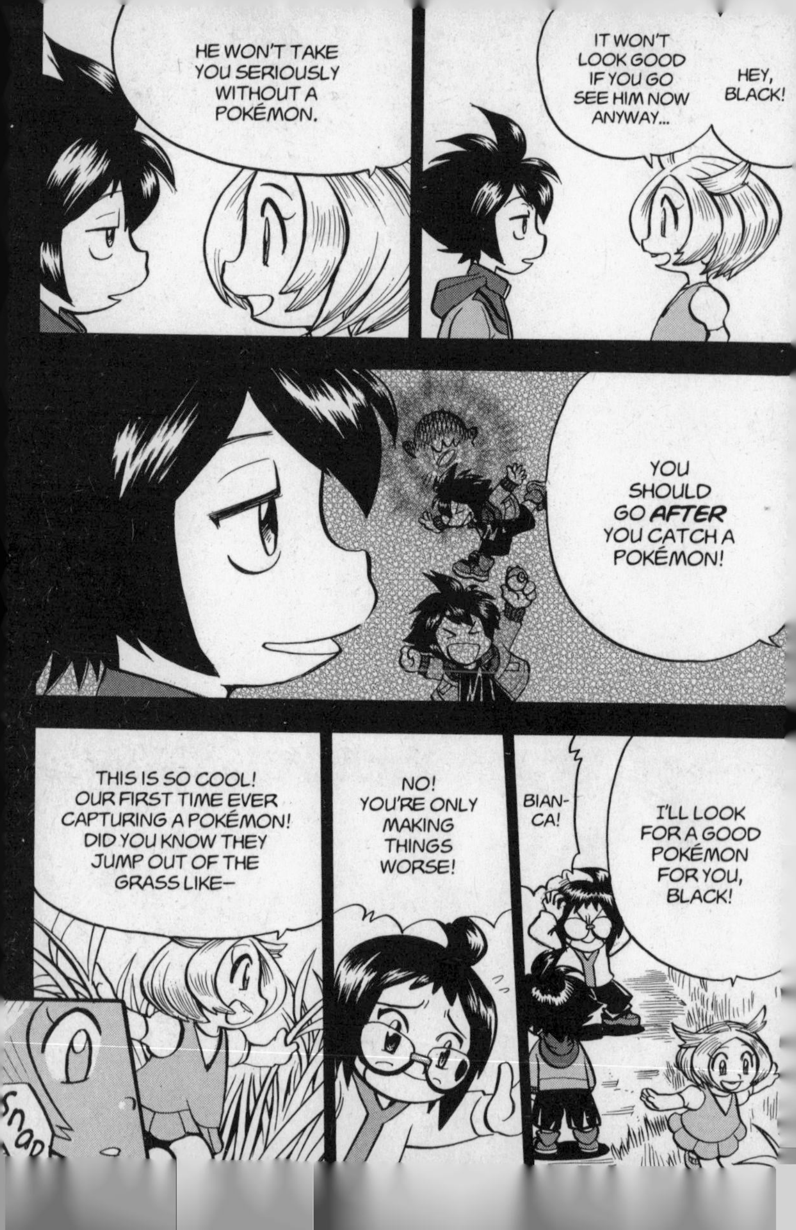
HEY, BLACK!
IT WON'T LOOK GOOD IF YOU GO SEE HIM NOW ANYWAY...
HE WON'T TAKE YOU SERIOUSLY WITHOUT A POKÉMON.
YOU SHOULD GO **AFTER** YOU CATCH A POKÉMON!
I'LL LOOK FOR A GOOD POKÉMON FOR YOU, BLACK!
BIAN-CA!
NO! YOU'RE ONLY MAKING THINGS WORSE!
THIS IS SO COOL! OUR FIRST TIME EVER CAPTURING A POKÉMON! DID YOU KNOW THEY JUMP OUT OF THE GRASS LIKE—

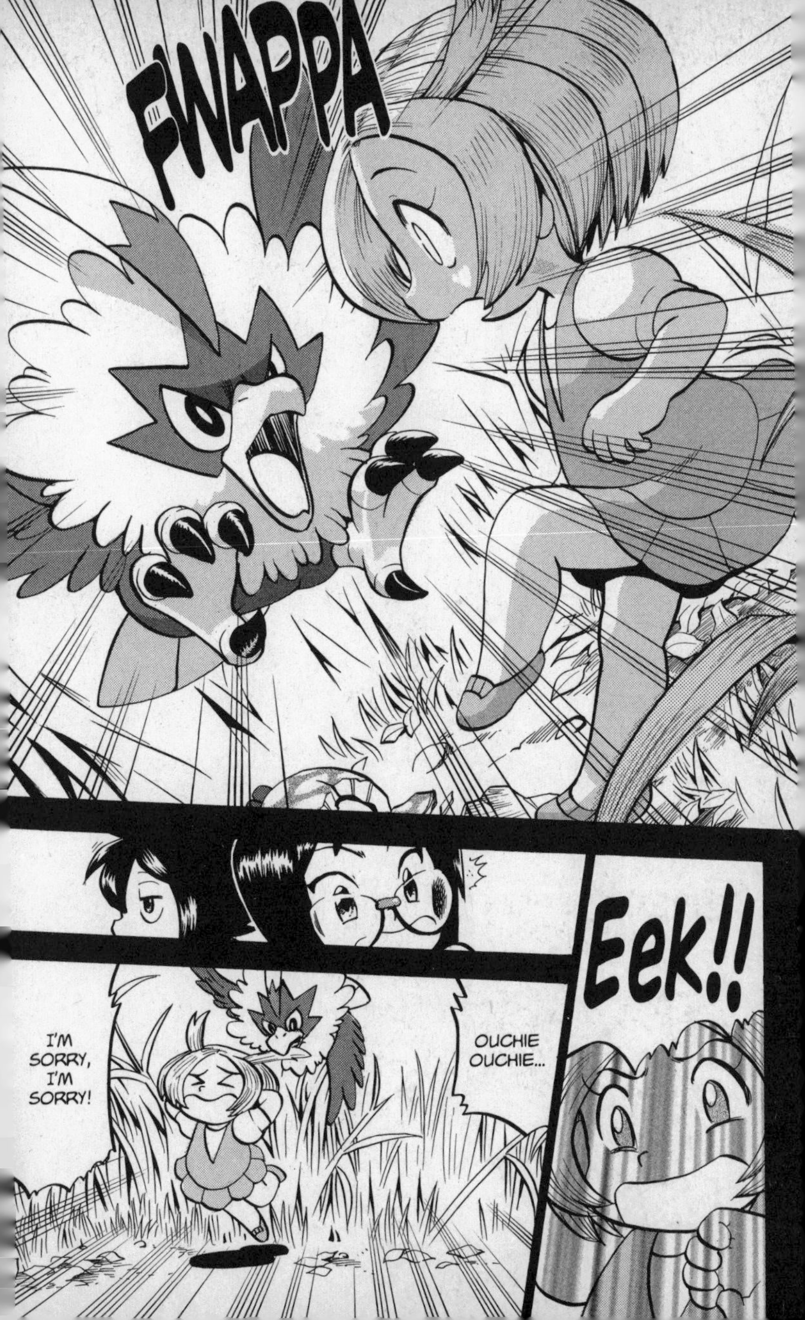
FWAPPA
Eek!!
OUCHIE OUCHIE...
I'M SORRY, I'M SORRY!

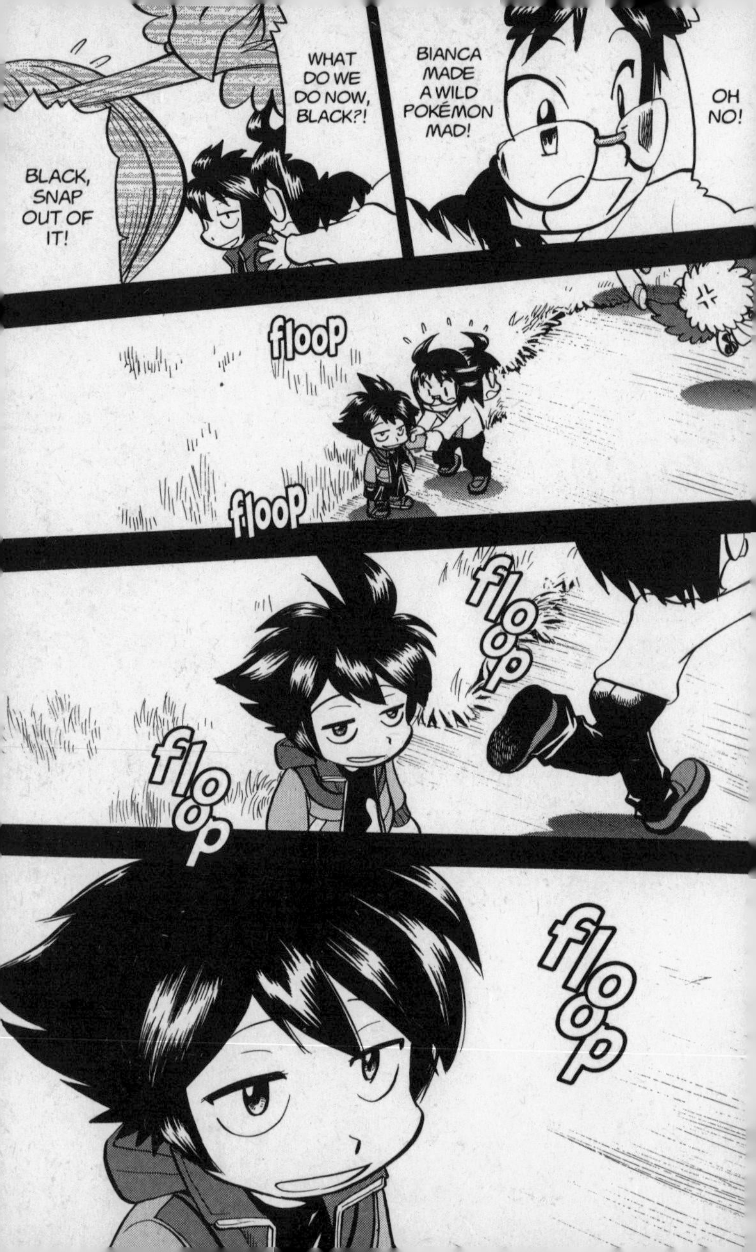
OH NO!
BIANCA MADE A WILD POKÉMON MAD!
WHAT DO WE DO NOW, BLACK?!
BLACK, SNAP OUT OF IT!
floop
floop
floop
floop
floop

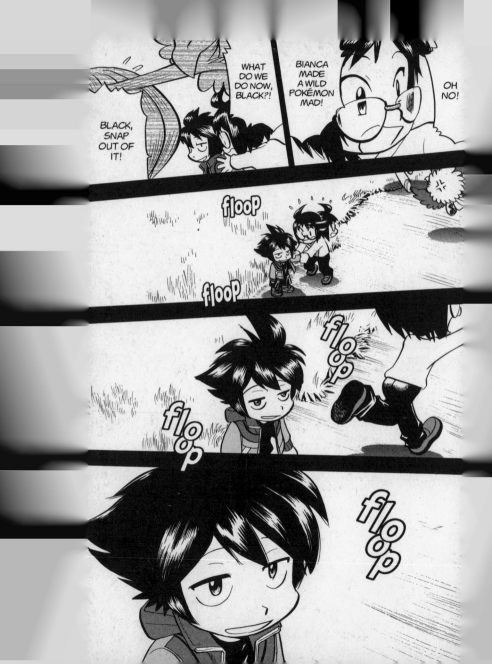

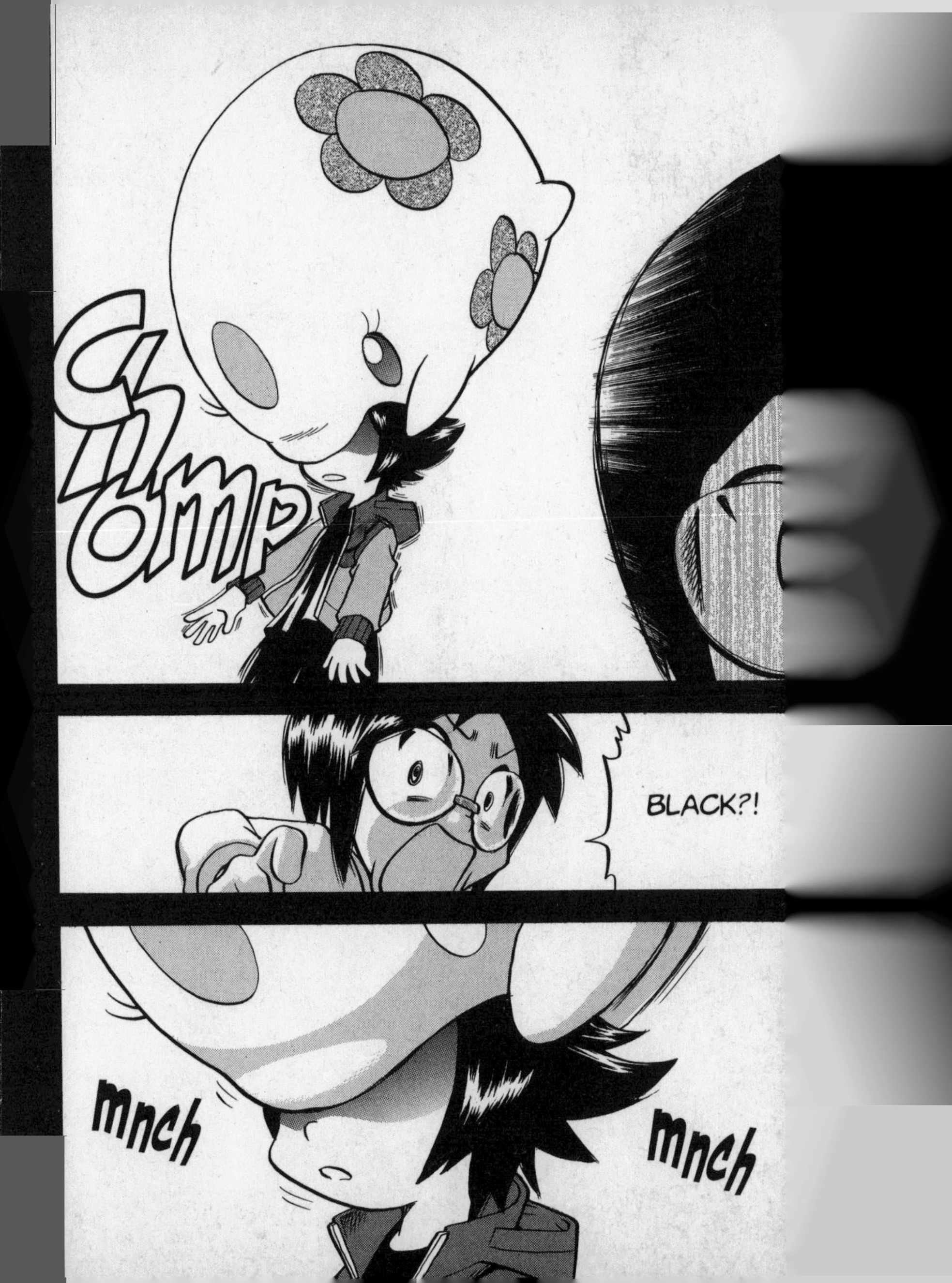
CHOMP
BLACK?!
mnch
mnch

Adventure 43
Tooth and Claw

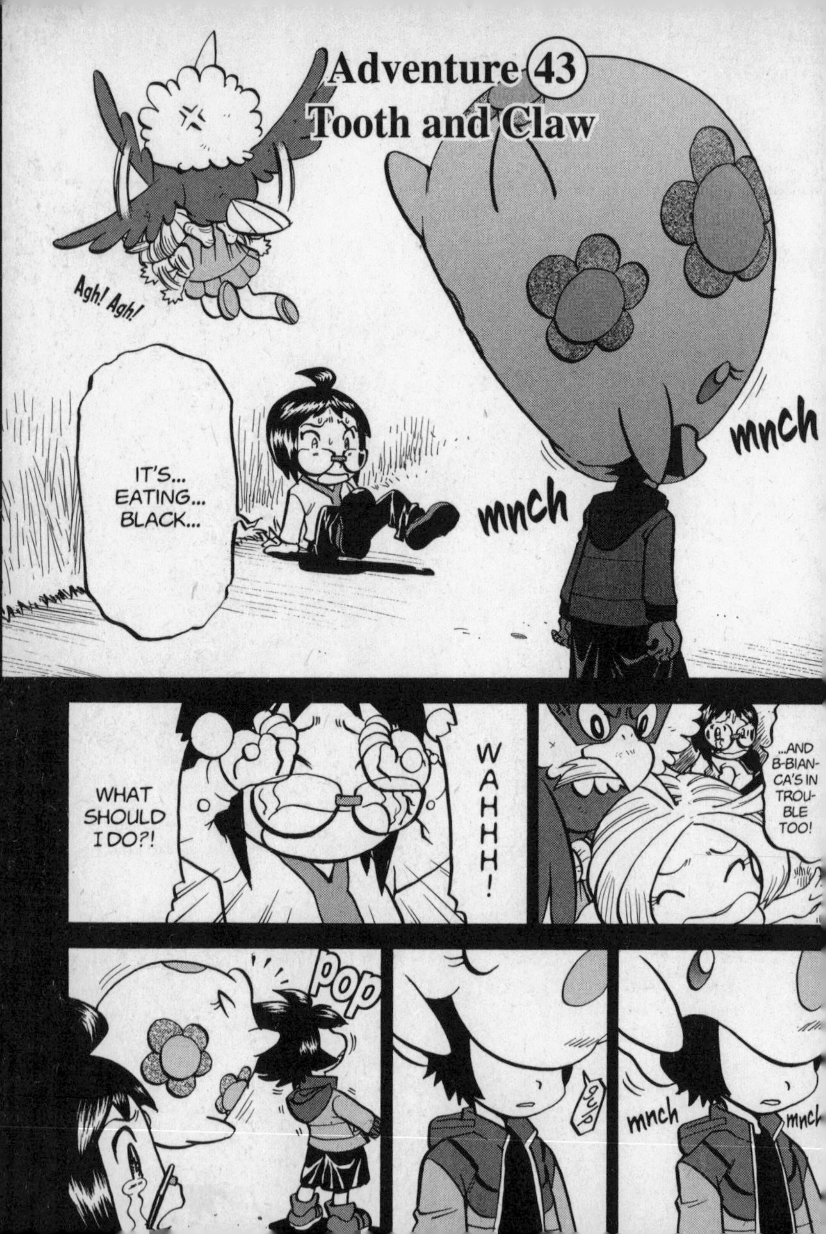
mnch
mnch
Agh! Agh!
IT'S... EATING... BLACK...
...AND B-BIANCA'S IN TROUBLE TOO!
WAHHH!
WHAT SHOULD I DO?!
mnch
mnch
pop

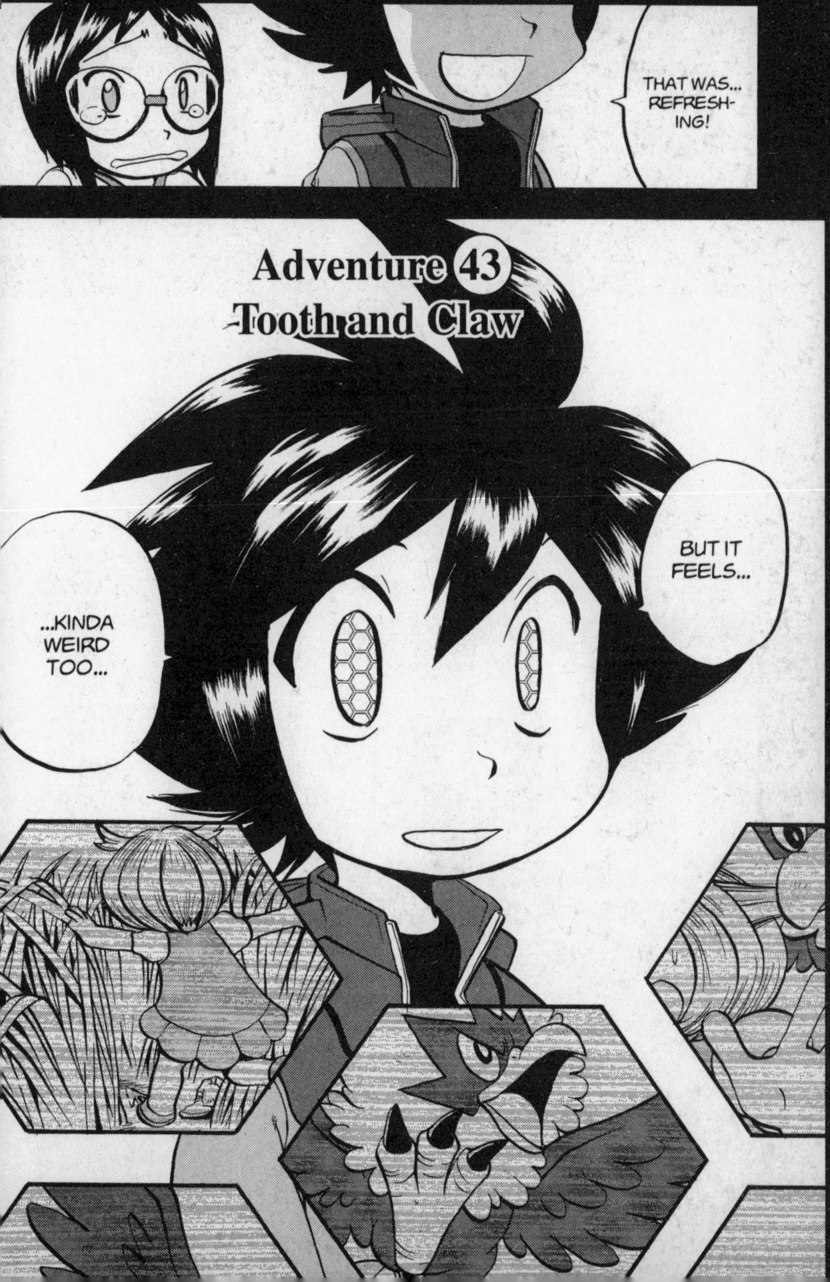
THAT WAS... REFRESH-ING!
Adventure 43
Tooth and Claw
BUT IT FEELS...
...KINDA WEIRD TOO...

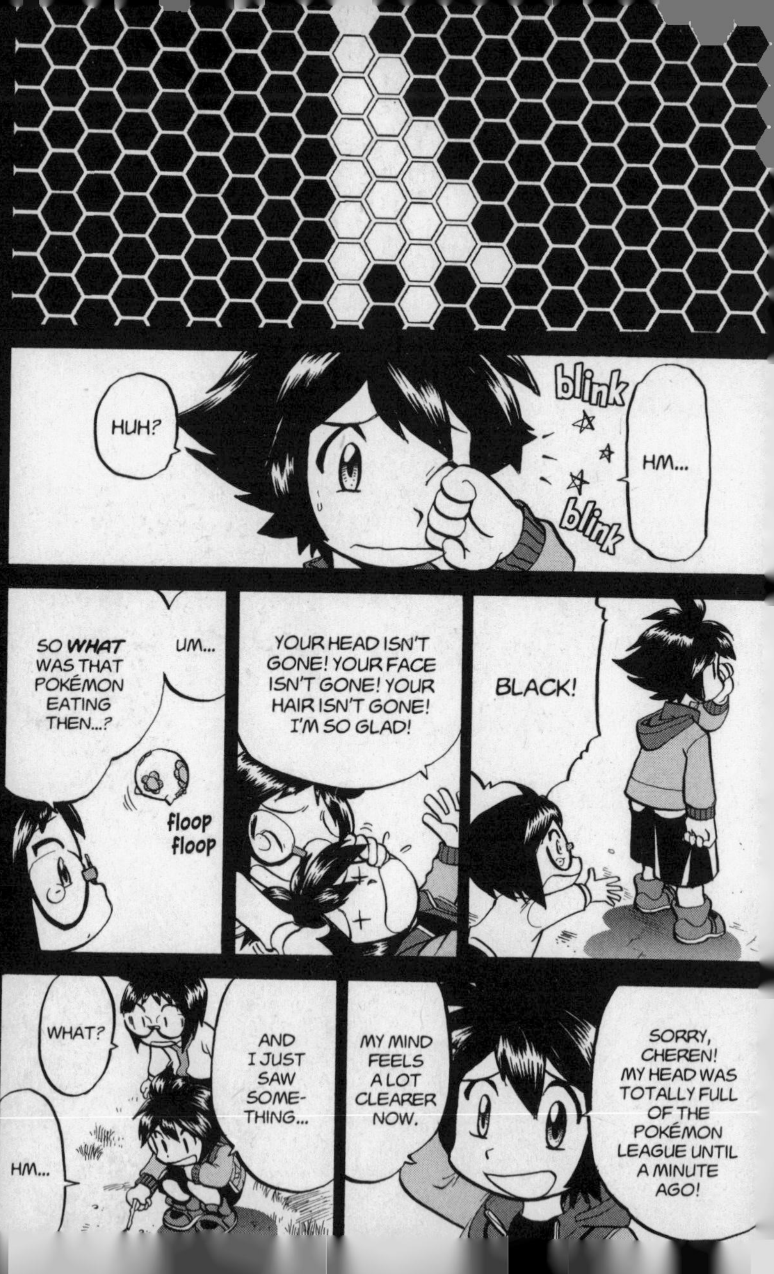
blink
HM...
blink
HUH?
BLACK!
YOUR HEAD ISN'T GONE! YOUR FACE ISN'T GONE! YOUR HAIR ISN'T GONE! I'M SO GLAD!
UM...
SO WHAT WAS THAT POKÉMON EATING THEN...?
floop floop
SORRY, CHEREN! MY HEAD WAS TOTALLY FULL OF THE POKÉMON LEAGUE UNTIL A MINUTE AGO!
MY MIND FEELS A LOT CLEARER NOW.
AND I JUST SAW SOME-THING...
WHAT?
HM...

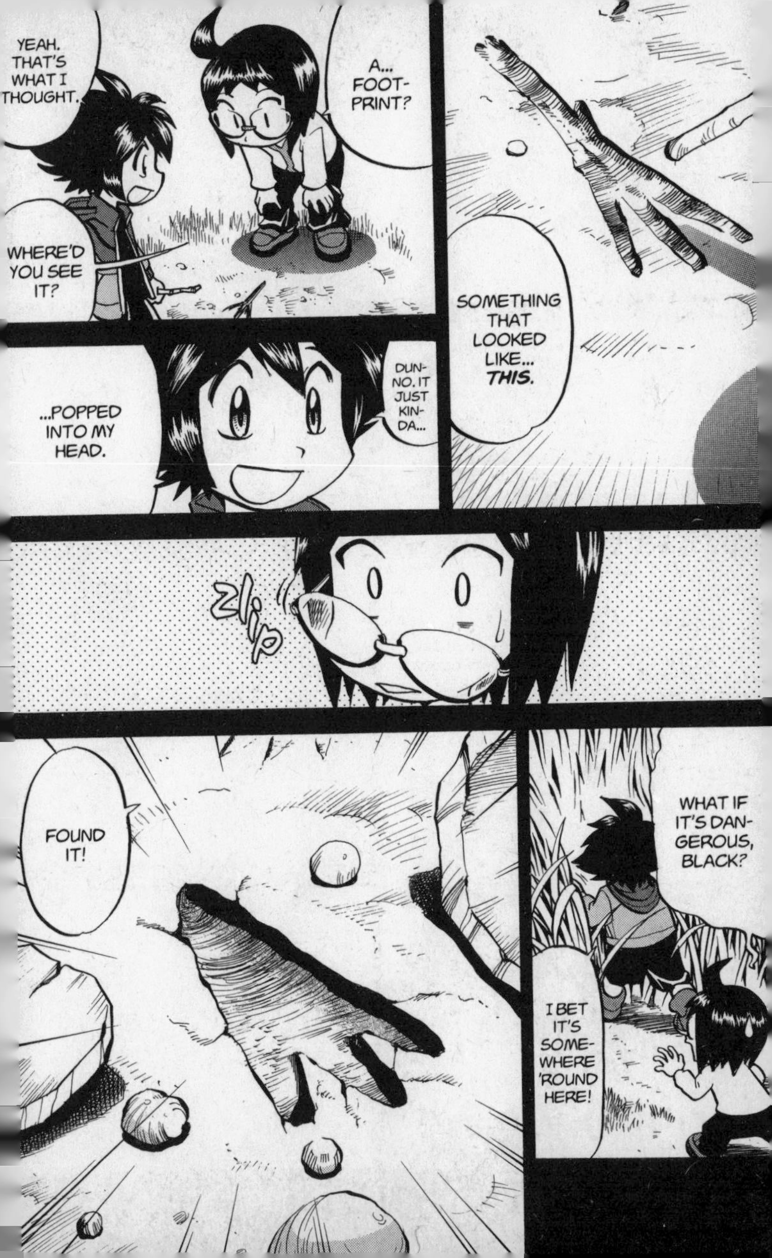
SOMETHING THAT LOOKED LIKE... THIS.
A... FOOT-PRINT?
YEAH. THAT'S WHAT I THOUGHT.
WHERE'D YOU SEE IT?
DUN-NO. IT JUST KIN-DA...
...POPPED INTO MY HEAD.
ZLIP
WHAT IF IT'S DAN-GEROUS, BLACK?
I BET IT'S SOME-WHERE 'ROUND HERE!
FOUND IT!

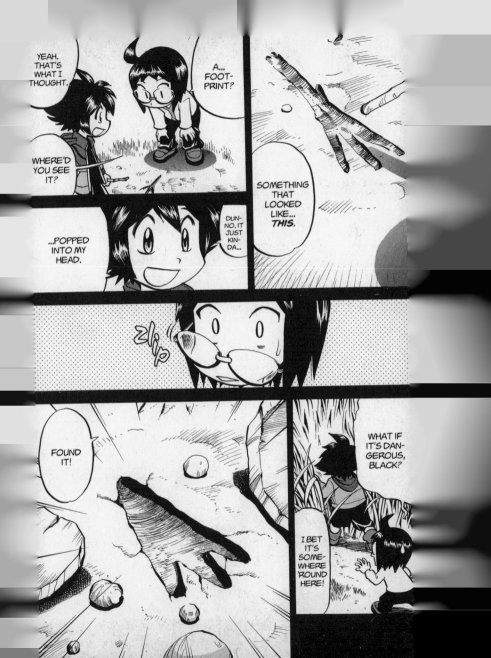

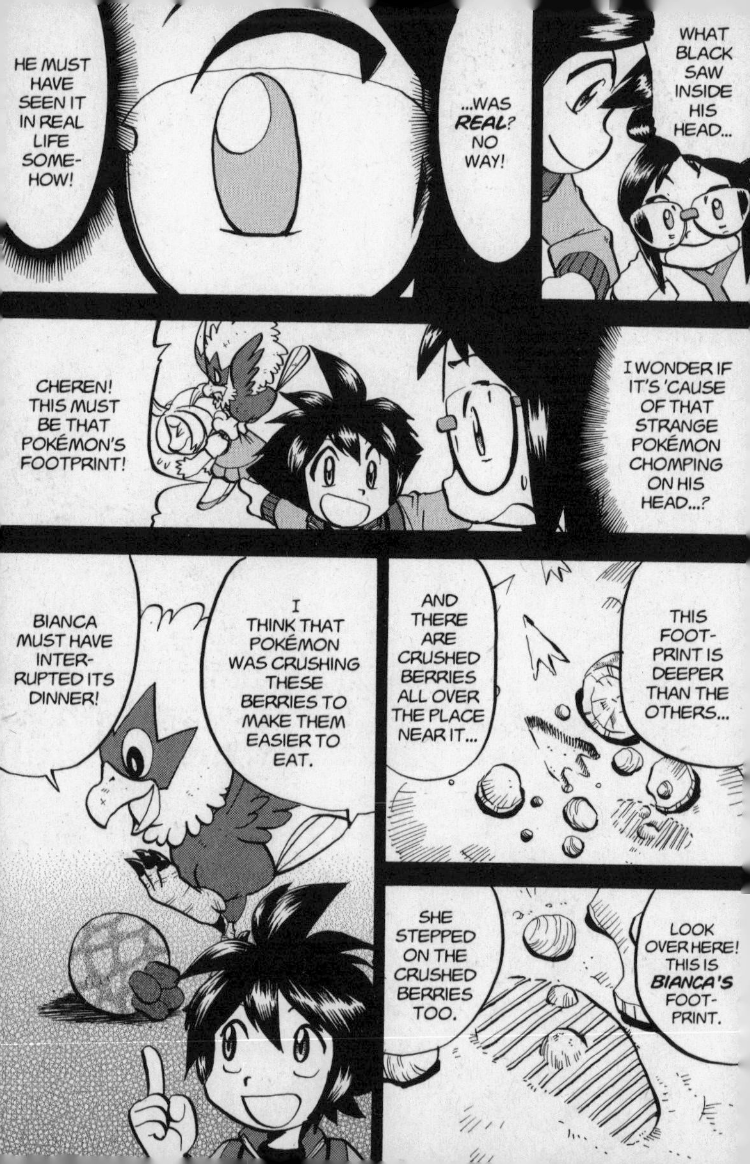
WHAT BLACK SAW INSIDE HIS HEAD...
...WAS **REAL**? NO WAY!
HE MUST HAVE SEEN IT IN REAL LIFE SOME-HOW!
I WONDER IF IT'S 'CAUSE OF THAT STRANGE POKÉMON CHOMPING ON HIS HEAD...?
CHEREN! THIS MUST BE THAT POKÉMON'S FOOTPRINT!
THIS FOOT-PRINT IS DEEPER THAN THE OTHERS...
AND THERE ARE CRUSHED BERRIES ALL OVER THE PLACE NEAR IT...
LOOK OVER HERE! THIS IS **BIANCA'S** FOOT-PRINT.
SHE STEPPED ON THE CRUSHED BERRIES TOO.
I THINK THAT POKÉMON WAS CRUSHING THESE BERRIES TO MAKE THEM EASIER TO EAT.
BIANCA MUST HAVE INTER-RUPTED ITS DINNER!

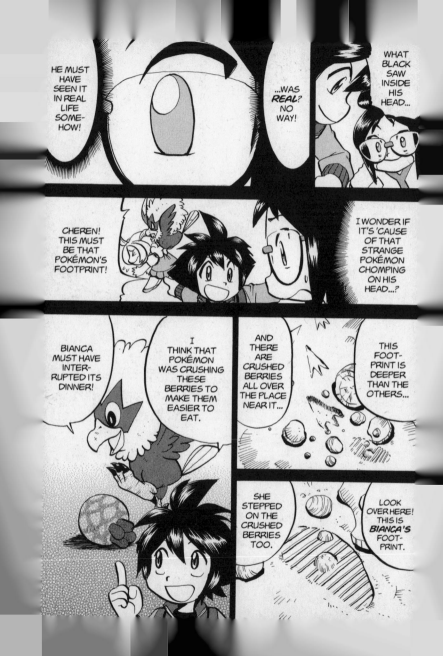

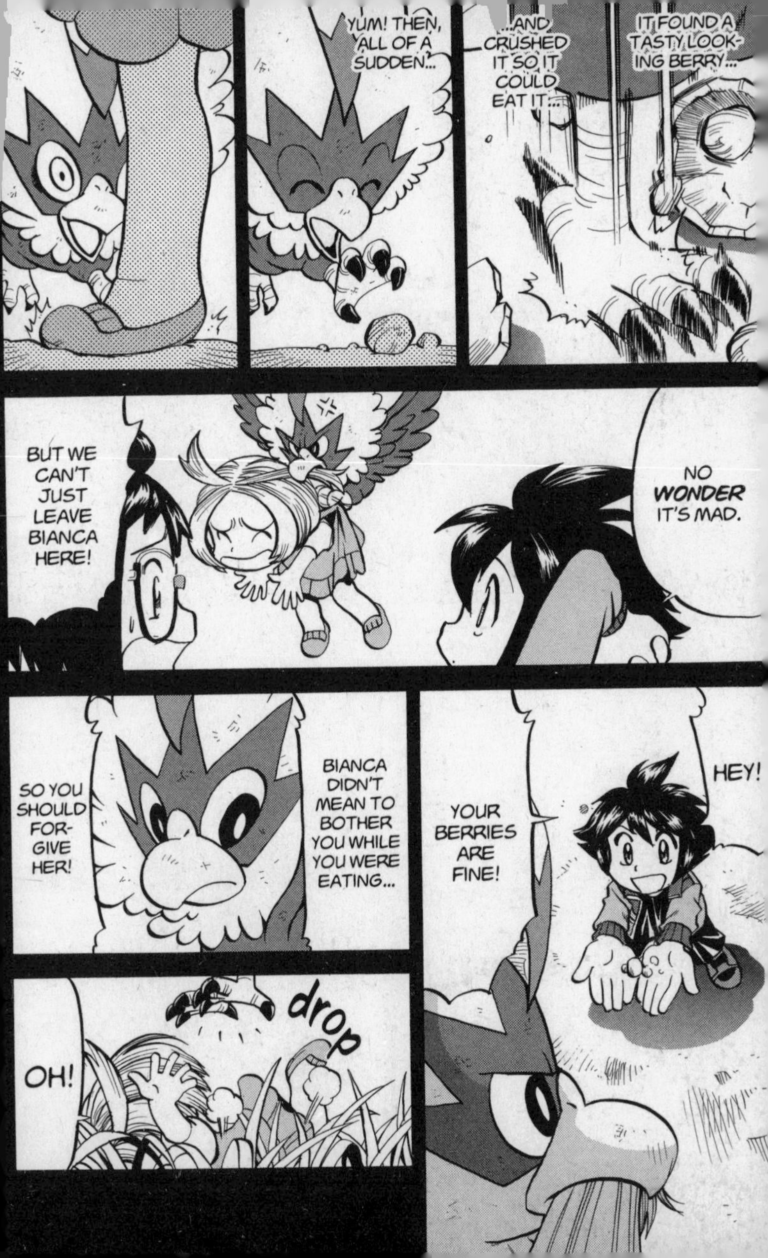

IT FOUND A TASTY LOOKING BERRY...
...AND CRUSHED IT SO IT COULD EAT IT...
YUM! THEN, ALL OF A SUDDEN...
NO WONDER IT'S MAD.
BUT WE CAN'T JUST LEAVE BIANCA HERE!
HEY!
YOUR BERRIES ARE FINE!
BIANCA DIDN'T MEAN TO BOTHER YOU WHILE YOU WERE EATING...
SO YOU SHOULD FORGIVE HER!
drop
OH!

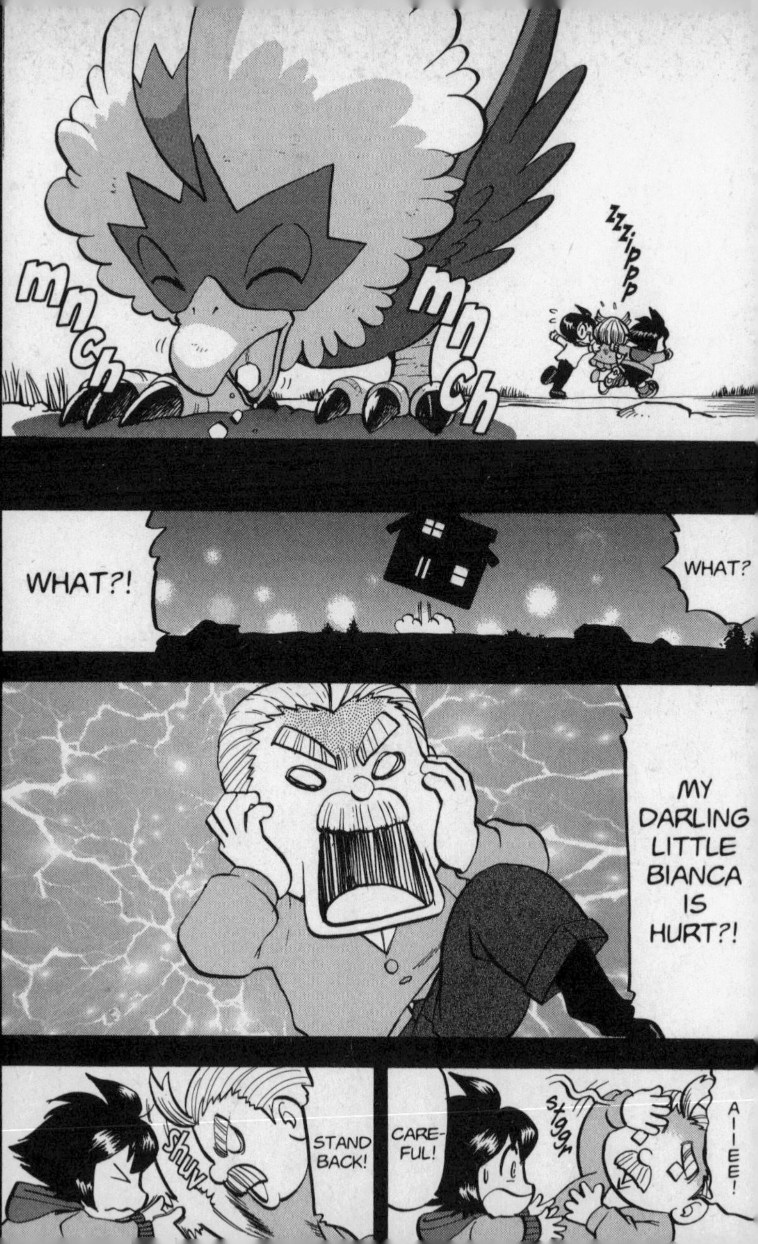
zzzippp
mnch
mnch
WHAT?
WHAT?!
MY DARLING LITTLE BIANCA IS HURT?!
AIIEE!
stggr
CARE-FUL!
STAND BACK!
shuv

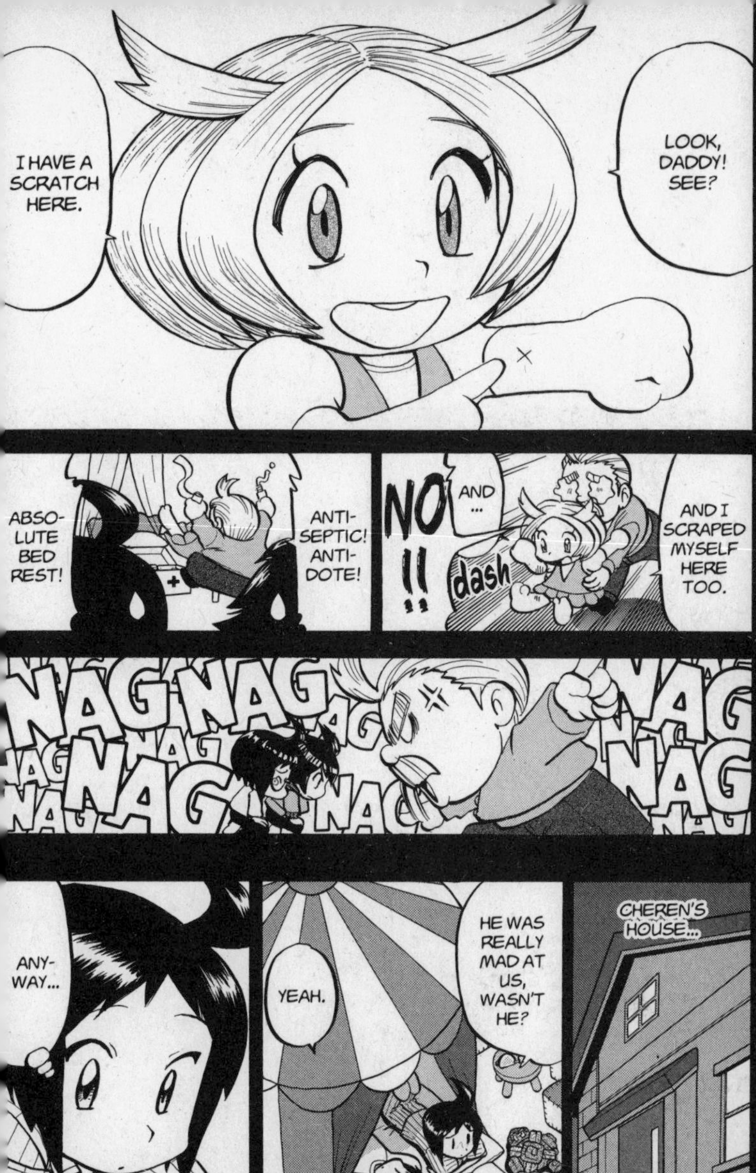
LOOK, DADDY! SEE?
I HAVE A SCRATCH HERE.
AND I SCRAPED MYSELF HERE TOO.
AND ...
dash
NO !!
ANTI-SEPTIC! ANTI-DOTE!
ABSO-LUTE BED REST!
NAG NAG NAG NAG NAG NAG NAG NAG NAG NAG
CHEREN'S HOUSE...
HE WAS REALLY MAD AT US, WASN'T HE?
YEAH.
ANY-WAY...

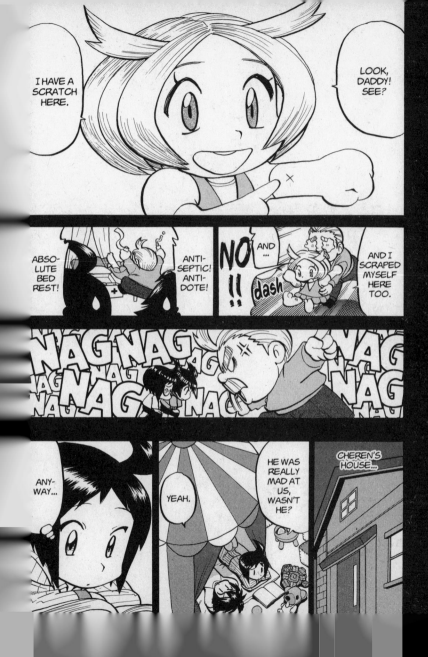

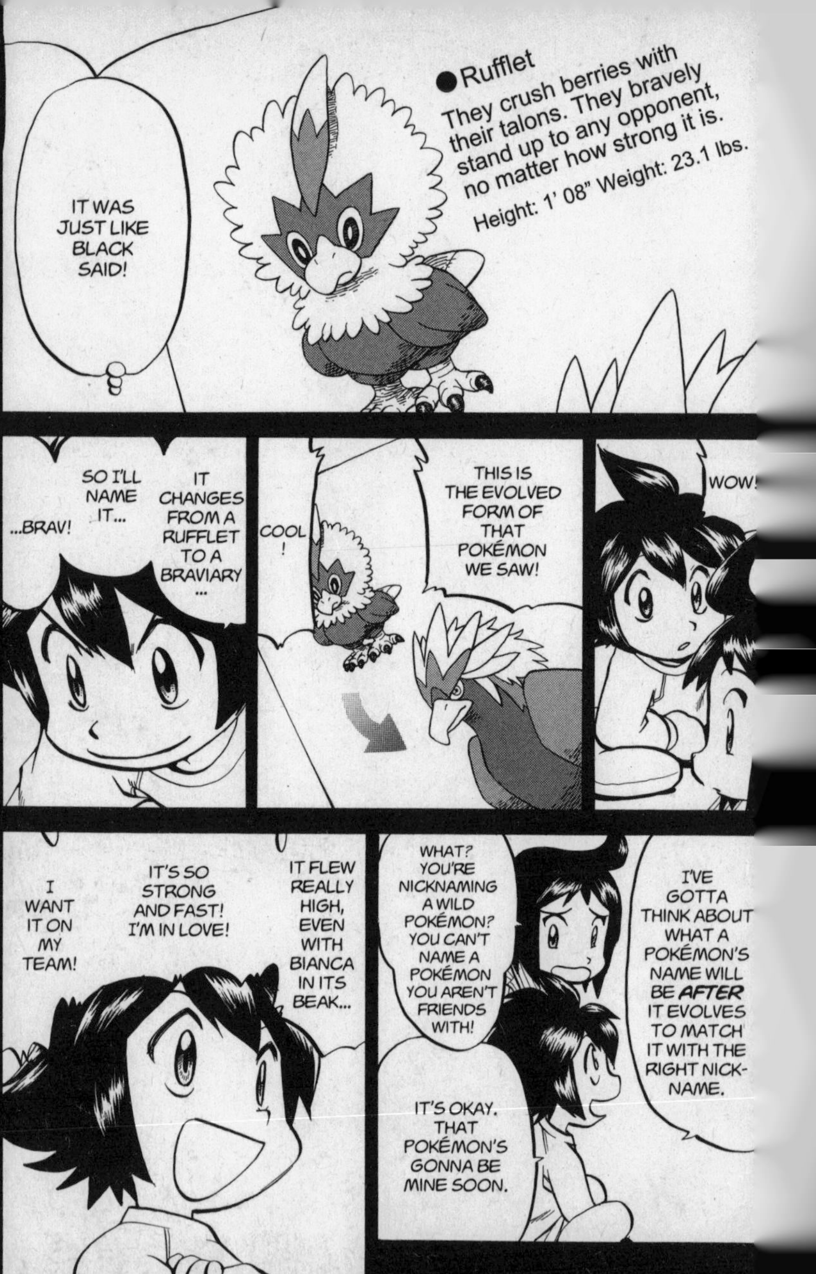
●Rufflet
They crush berries with their talons. They bravely stand up to any opponent, no matter how strong it is.
Height: 1' 08" Weight: 23.1 lbs.
IT WAS JUST LIKE BLACK SAID!
WOW!
THIS IS THE EVOLVED FORM OF THAT POKÉMON WE SAW!
COOL!
IT CHANGES FROM A RUFFLET TO A BRAVIARY...
SO I'LL NAME IT...
...BRAV!
I'VE GOTTA THINK ABOUT WHAT A POKÉMON'S NAME WILL BE *AFTER* IT EVOLVES TO MATCH IT WITH THE RIGHT NICK-NAME.
WHAT? YOU'RE NICKNAMING A WILD POKÉMON? YOU CAN'T NAME A POKÉMON YOU AREN'T FRIENDS WITH!
IT'S OKAY. THAT POKÉMON'S GONNA BE MINE SOON.
IT FLEW REALLY HIGH, EVEN WITH BIANCA IN ITS BEAK...
IT'S SO STRONG AND FAST! I'M IN LOVE!
I WANT IT ON MY TEAM!

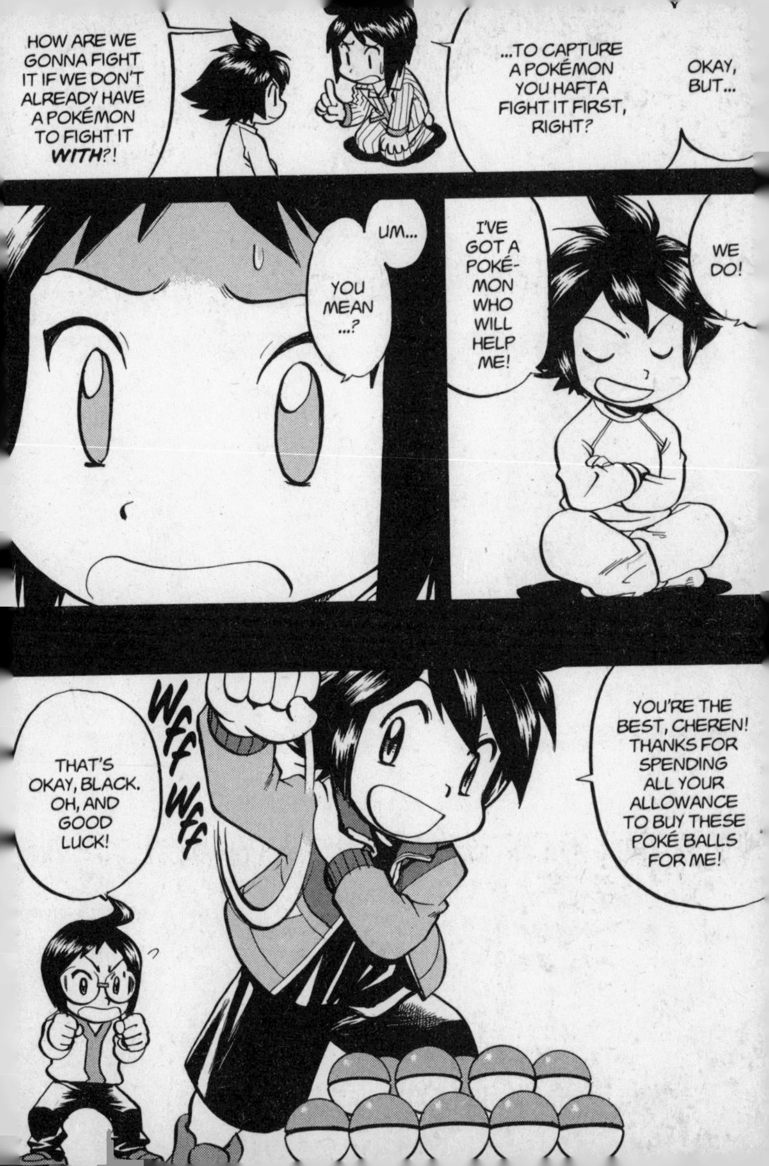
OKAY, BUT...
...TO CAPTURE A POKÉMON YOU HAFTA FIGHT IT FIRST, RIGHT?
HOW ARE WE GONNA FIGHT IT IF WE DON'T ALREADY HAVE A POKÉMON TO FIGHT IT **WITH**?!
WE DO!
I'VE GOT A POKÉ-MON WHO WILL HELP ME!
UM...
YOU MEAN ...?
YOU'RE THE BEST, CHEREN! THANKS FOR SPENDING ALL YOUR ALLOWANCE TO BUY THESE POKÉ BALLS FOR ME!
WFF WFF
THAT'S OKAY, BLACK. OH, AND GOOD LUCK!

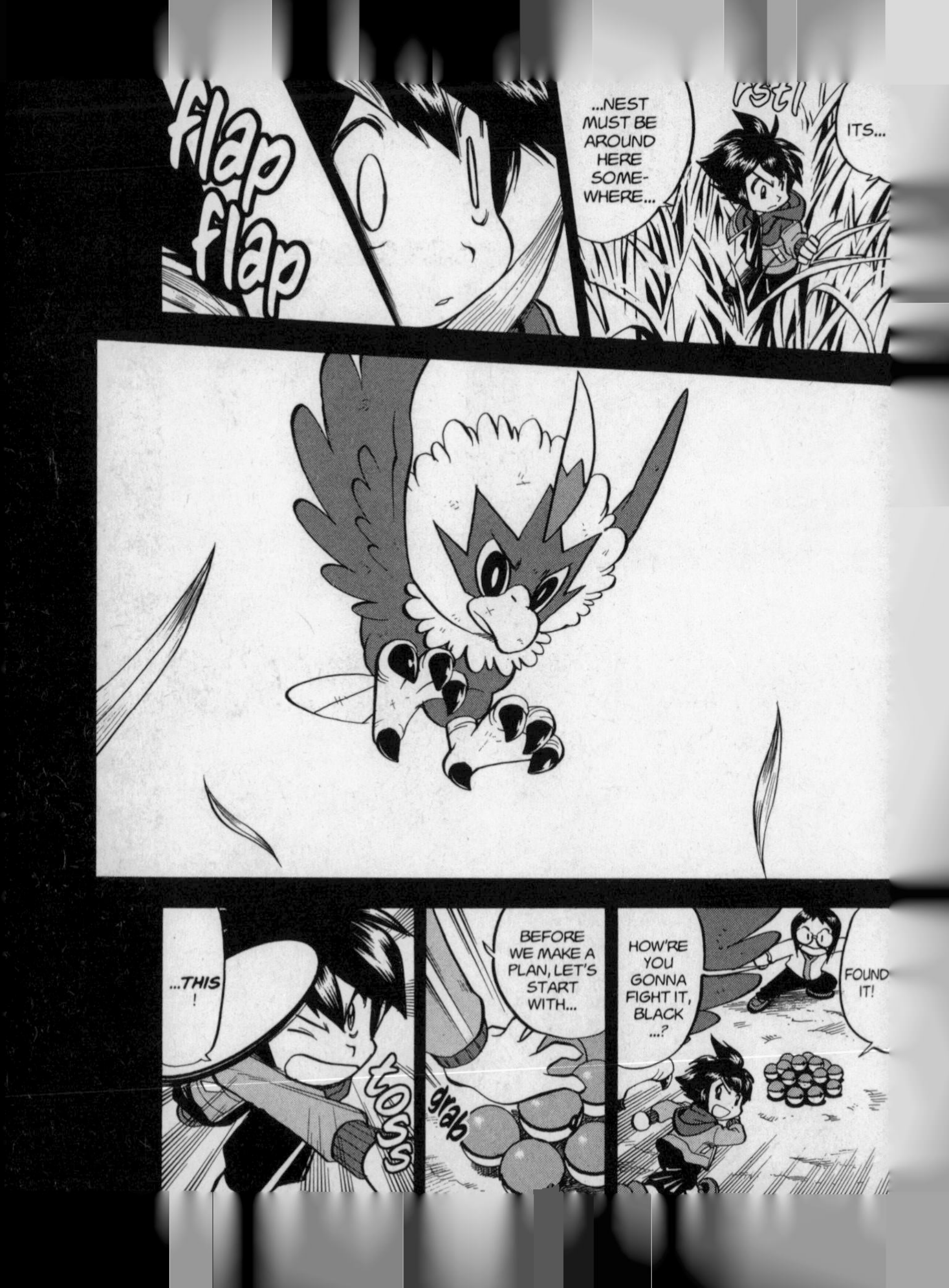
rstl
ITS...
...NEST MUST BE AROUND HERE SOME-WHERE...
flap flap
FOUND IT!
HOW'RE YOU GONNA FIGHT IT, BLACK ...?
BEFORE WE MAKE A PLAN, LET'S START WITH...
grab
...THIS!
toss

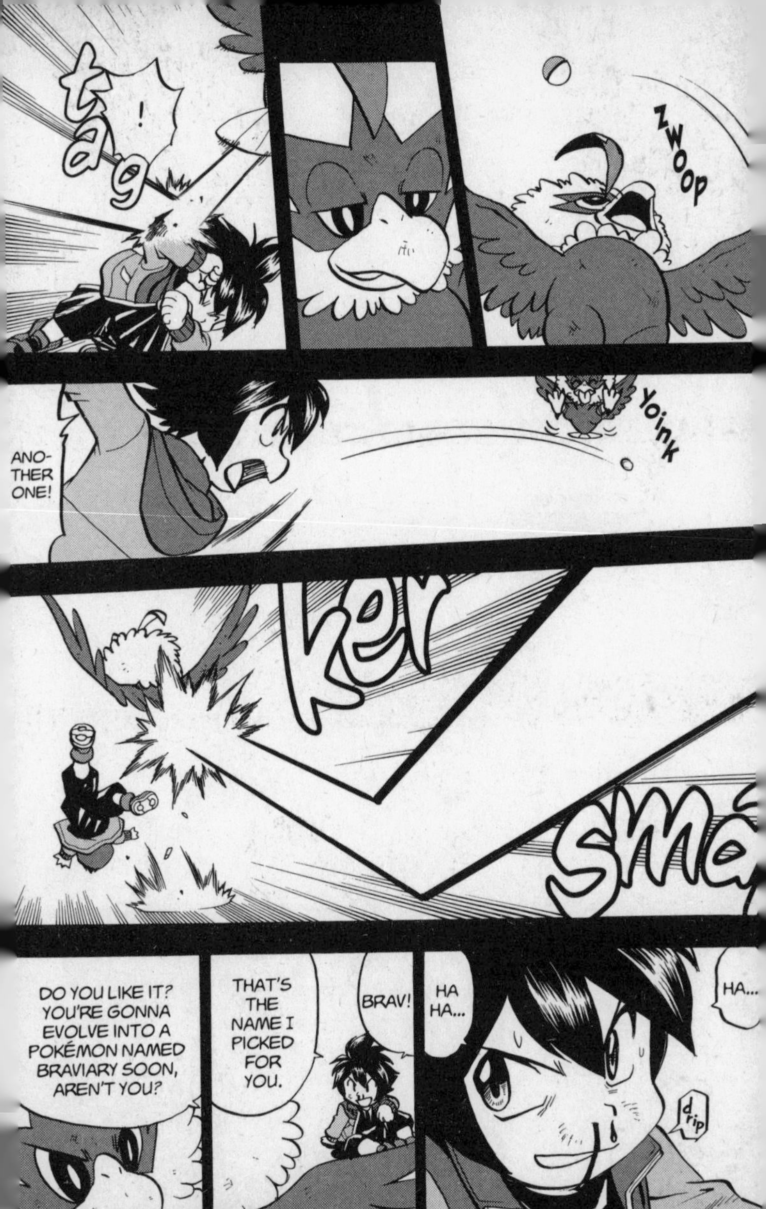

ZWOOP
tag
!
Yoink
ANO-
THER
ONE!
ker
sma
HA...
HA
HA...
drip
BRAV!
THAT'S THE NAME I PICKED FOR YOU.
DO YOU LIKE IT? YOU'RE GONNA EVOLVE INTO A POKÉMON NAMED BRAVIARY SOON, AREN'T YOU?

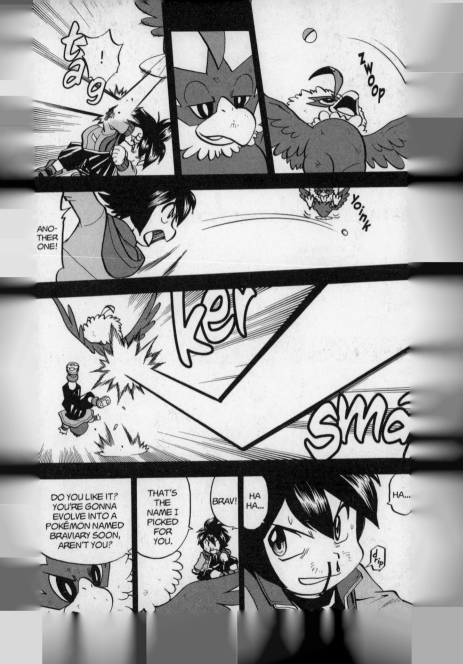

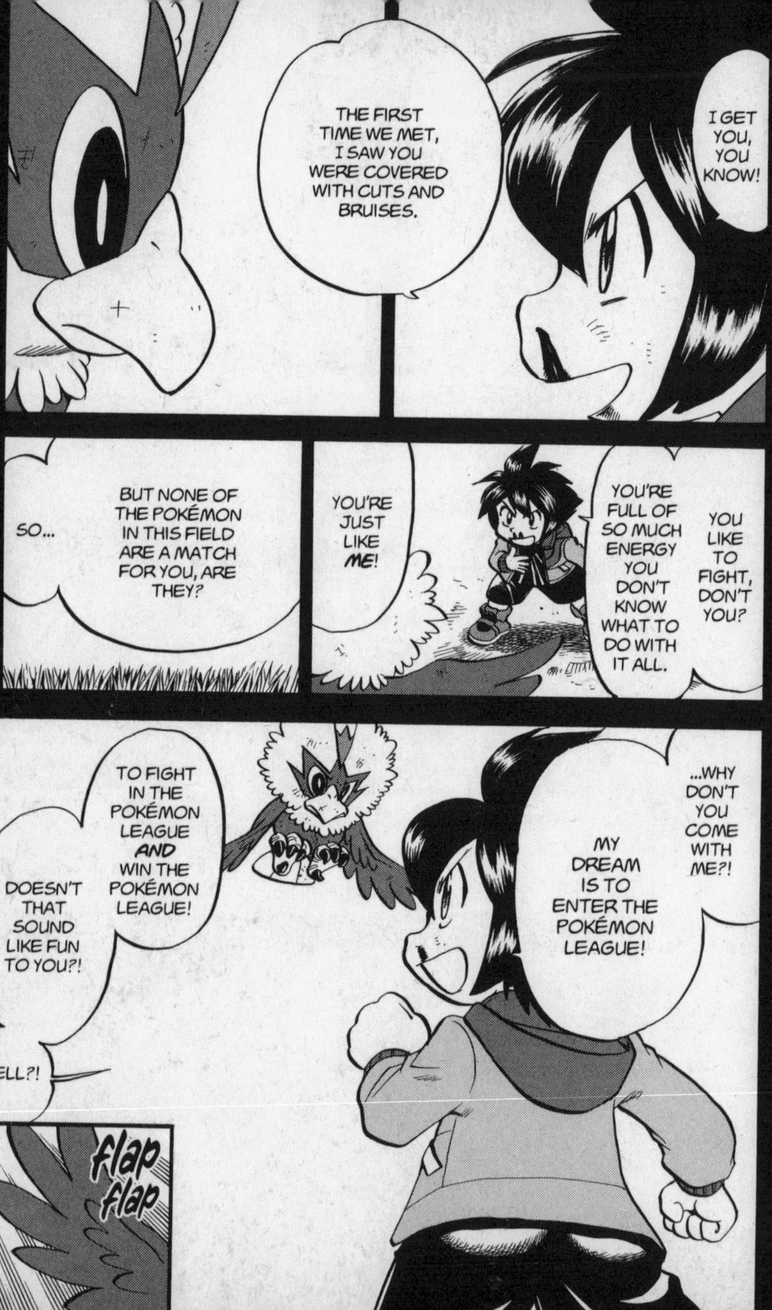
I GET YOU, YOU KNOW!
THE FIRST TIME WE MET, I SAW YOU WERE COVERED WITH CUTS AND BRUISES.
YOU LIKE TO FIGHT, DON'T YOU?
YOU'RE FULL OF SO MUCH ENERGY YOU DON'T KNOW WHAT TO DO WITH IT ALL.
YOU'RE JUST LIKE *ME*!
BUT NONE OF THE POKÉMON IN THIS FIELD ARE A MATCH FOR YOU, ARE THEY?
SO...
...WHY DON'T YOU COME WITH ME?!
MY DREAM IS TO ENTER THE POKÉMON LEAGUE!
TO FIGHT IN THE POKÉMON LEAGUE *AND* WIN THE POKÉMON LEAGUE!
DOESN'T THAT SOUND LIKE FUN TO YOU?!
WELL?!
flap flap

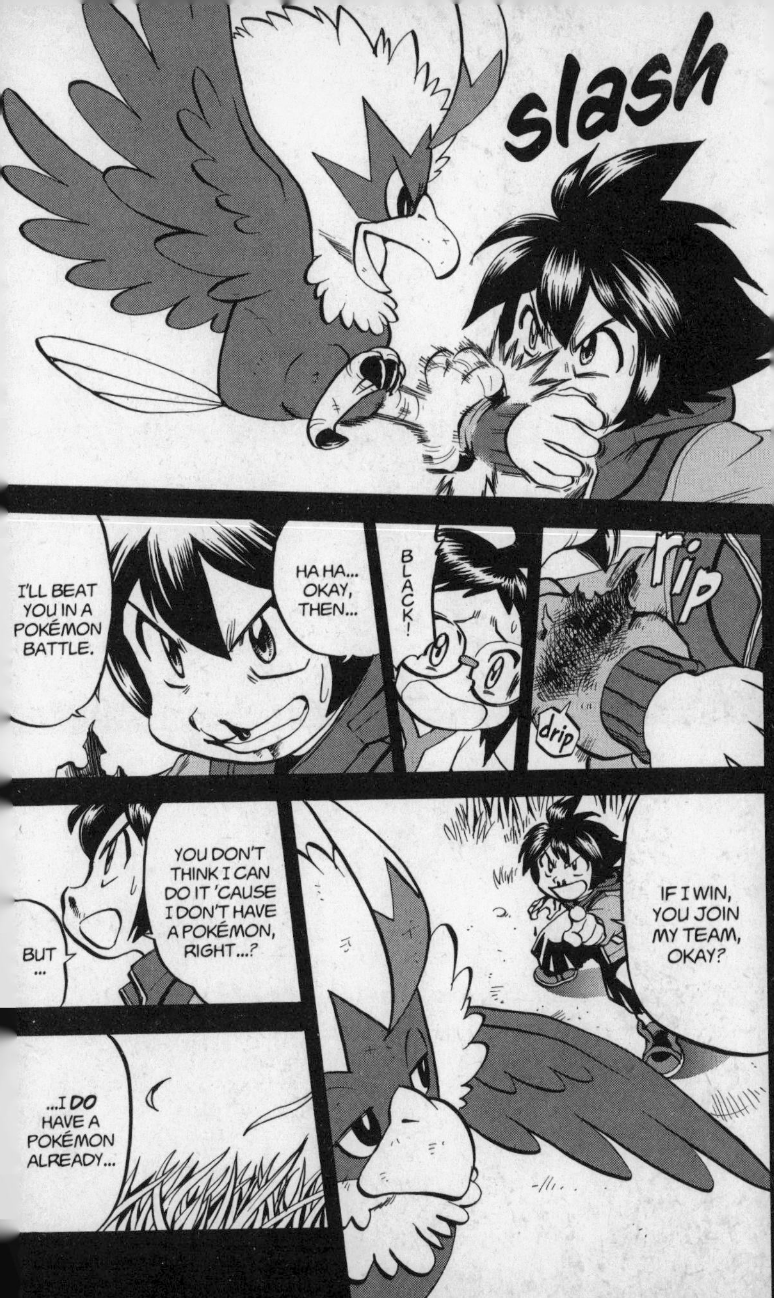
slash
rip
drip
BLACK!
HA HA... OKAY, THEN...
I'LL BEAT YOU IN A POKÉMON BATTLE.
IF I WIN, YOU JOIN MY TEAM, OKAY?
YOU DON'T THINK I CAN DO IT 'CAUSE I DON'T HAVE A POKÉMON, RIGHT...?
BUT ...
...I **DO** HAVE A POKÉMON ALREADY...

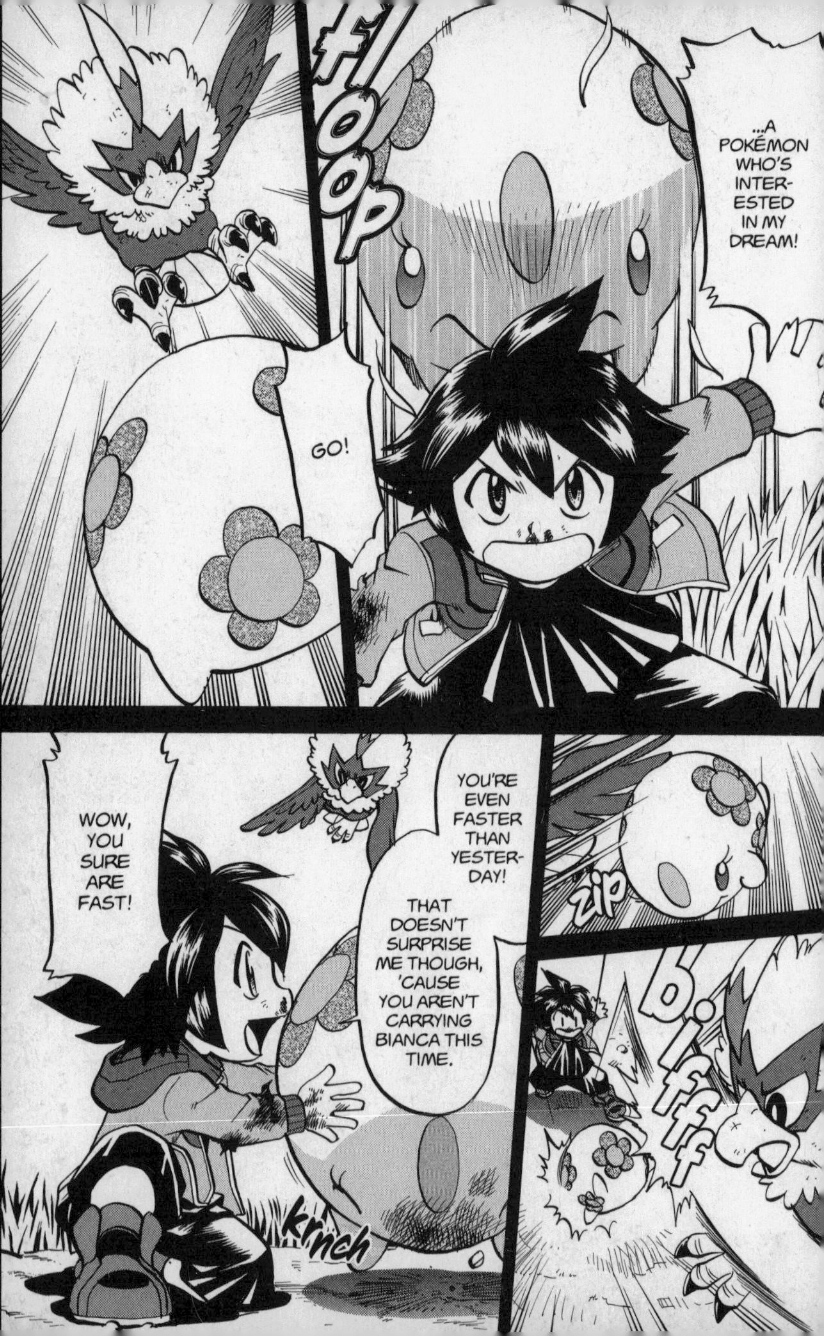
...A POKÉMON WHO'S INTER-ESTED IN MY DREAM!
GO!
FWOOOP
zip
biffff
YOU'RE EVEN FASTER THAN YESTER-DAY!
THAT DOESN'T SURPRISE ME THOUGH, 'CAUSE YOU AREN'T CARRYING BIANCA THIS TIME.
WOW, YOU SURE ARE FAST!
krnch

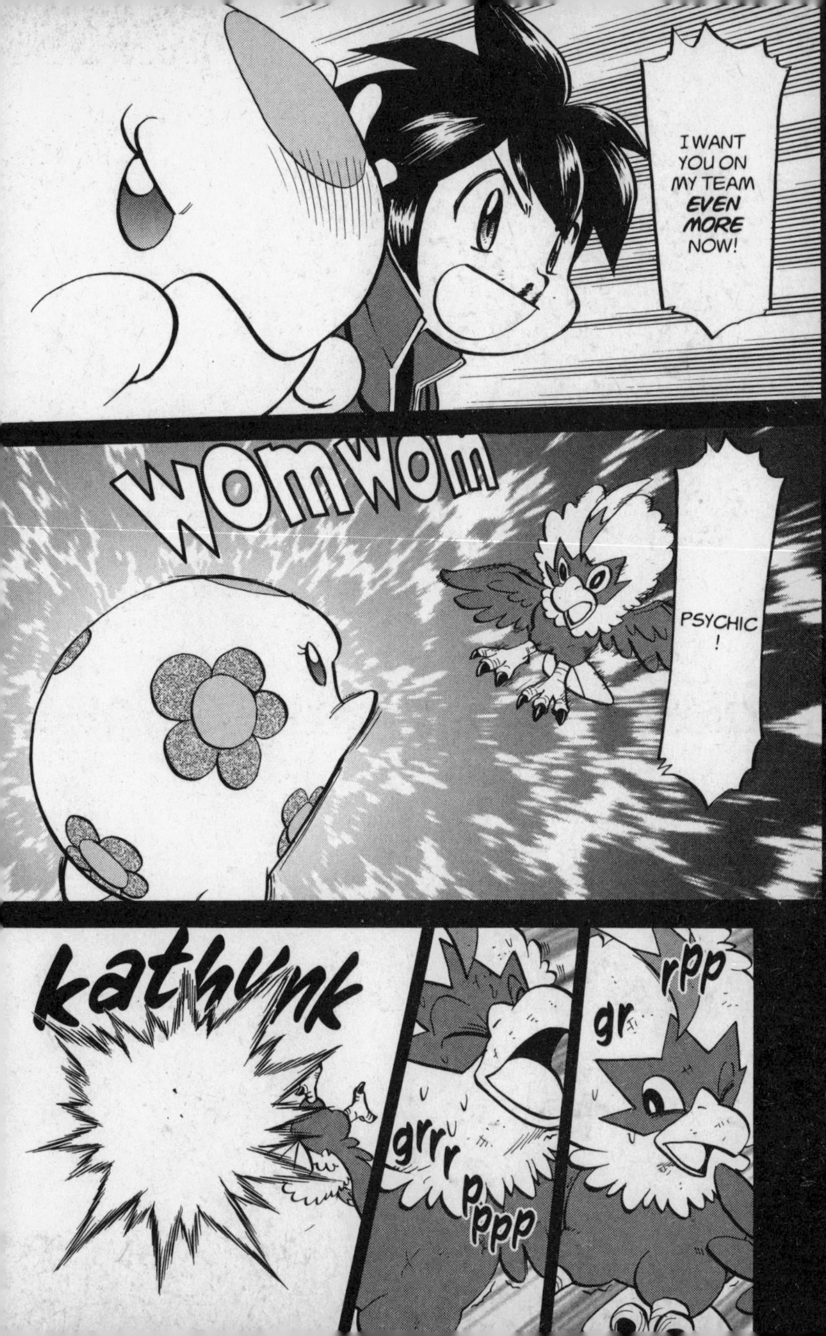
I WANT YOU ON MY TEAM **EVEN MORE** NOW!
PSYCHIC!
WOMWOM
rpp
gr
grrr
pppp
kathunk

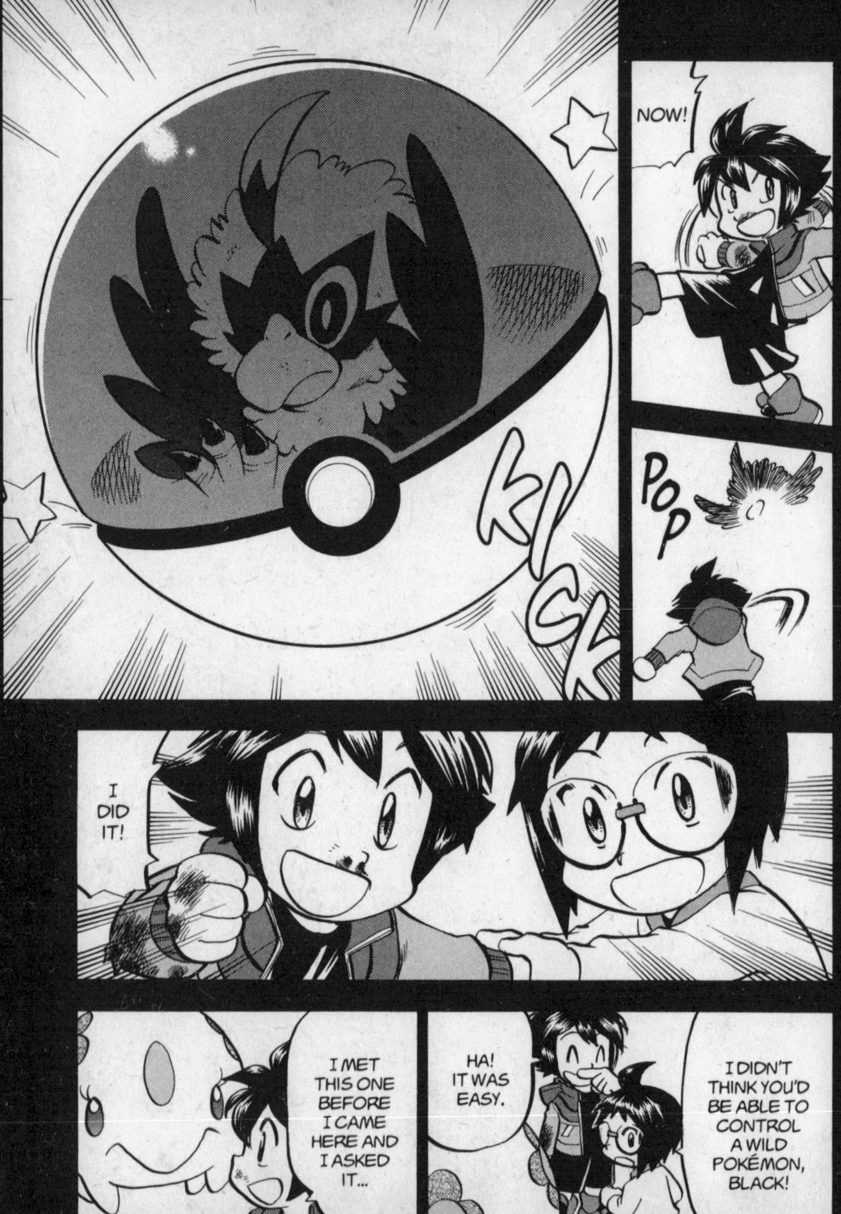
NOW!
POP
KICK
I DID IT!
I DIDN'T THINK YOU'D BE ABLE TO CONTROL A WILD POKÉMON, BLACK!
HA! IT WAS EASY.
I MET THIS ONE BEFORE I CAME HERE AND I ASKED IT...

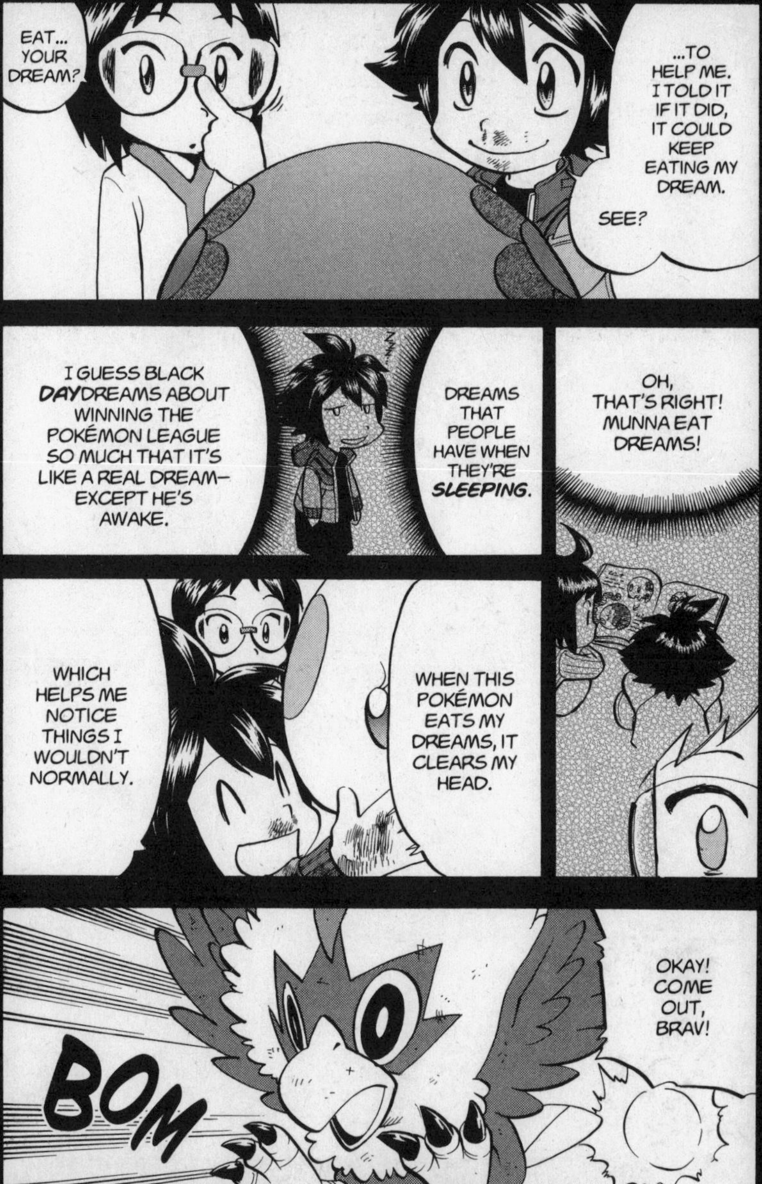
...TO HELP ME. I TOLD IT IF IT DID, IT COULD KEEP EATING MY DREAM.
SEE?
EAT... YOUR DREAM?
OH, THAT'S RIGHT! MUNNA EAT DREAMS!
DREAMS THAT PEOPLE HAVE WHEN THEY'RE *SLEEPING*.
I GUESS BLACK ***DAY***DREAMS ABOUT WINNING THE POKÉMON LEAGUE SO MUCH THAT IT'S LIKE A REAL DREAM—EXCEPT HE'S AWAKE.
WHEN THIS POKÉMON EATS MY DREAMS, IT CLEARS MY HEAD.
WHICH HELPS ME NOTICE THINGS I WOULDN'T NORMALLY.
OKAY! COME OUT, BRAV!
BOM

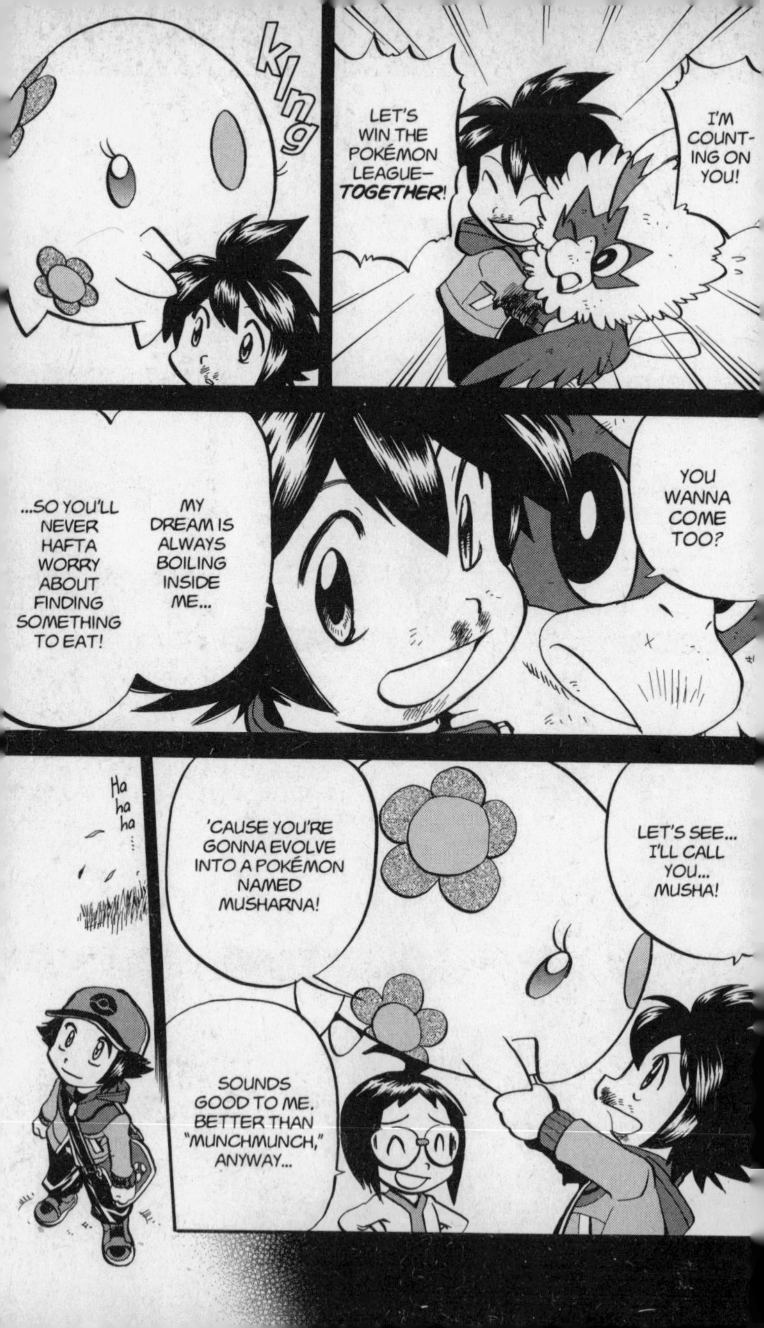
I'M COUNTING ON YOU!
LET'S WIN THE POKÉMON LEAGUE—**TOGETHER**!
kling
YOU WANNA COME TOO?
MY DREAM IS ALWAYS BOILING INSIDE ME...
...SO YOU'LL NEVER HAFTA WORRY ABOUT FINDING SOMETHING TO EAT!
LET'S SEE... I'LL CALL YOU... MUSHA!
'CAUSE YOU'RE GONNA EVOLVE INTO A POKÉMON NAMED MUSHARNA!
SOUNDS GOOD TO ME. BETTER THAN "MUNCHMUNCH," ANYWAY...
Ha ha ha...

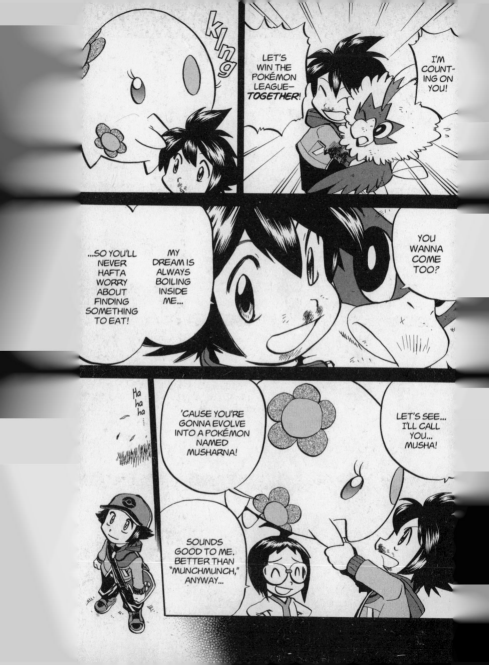

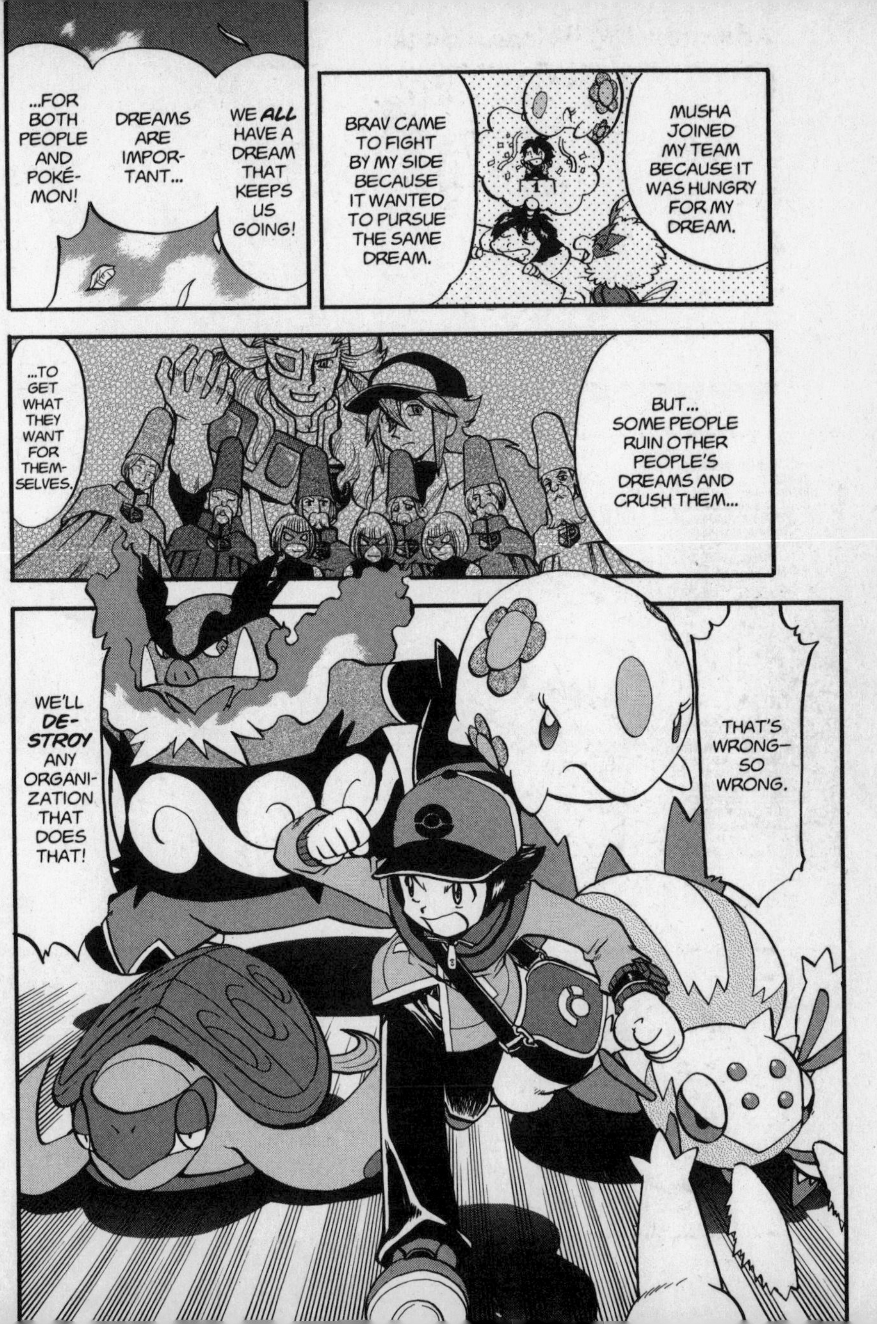
MUSHA JOINED MY TEAM BECAUSE IT WAS HUNGRY FOR MY DREAM.
BRAV CAME TO FIGHT BY MY SIDE BECAUSE IT WANTED TO PURSUE THE SAME DREAM.
WE **ALL** HAVE A DREAM THAT KEEPS US GOING!
DREAMS ARE IMPORTANT...
...FOR BOTH PEOPLE AND POKÉMON!
BUT... SOME PEOPLE RUIN OTHER PEOPLE'S DREAMS AND CRUSH THEM...
...TO GET WHAT THEY WANT FOR THEMSELVES.
THAT'S WRONG—SO WRONG.
WE'LL **DESTROY** ANY ORGANIZATION THAT DOES THAT!

Adventure 44 Welcome Home

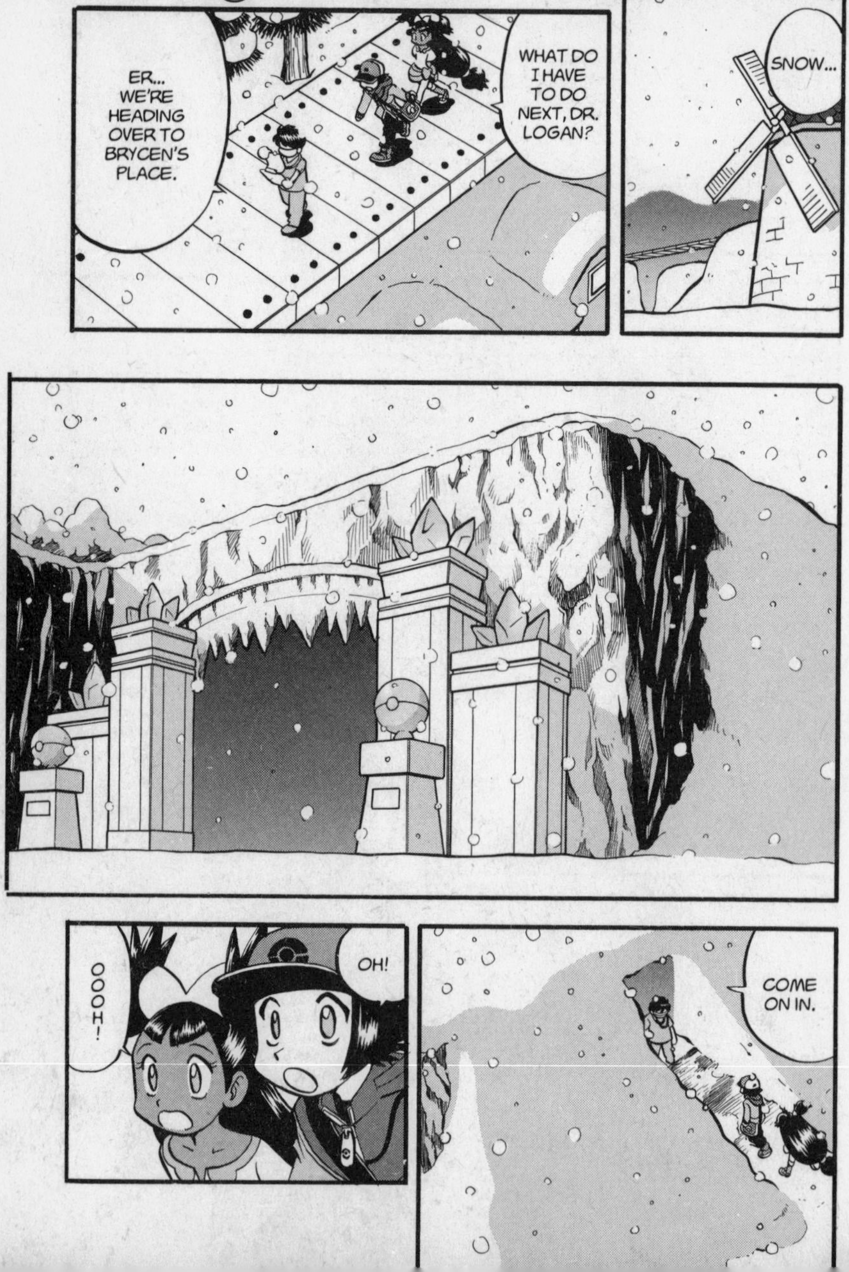
SNOW...
WHAT DO I HAVE TO DO NEXT, DR. LOGAN?
ER... WE'RE HEADING OVER TO BRYCEN'S PLACE.
COME ON IN.
OH!
OOOH!

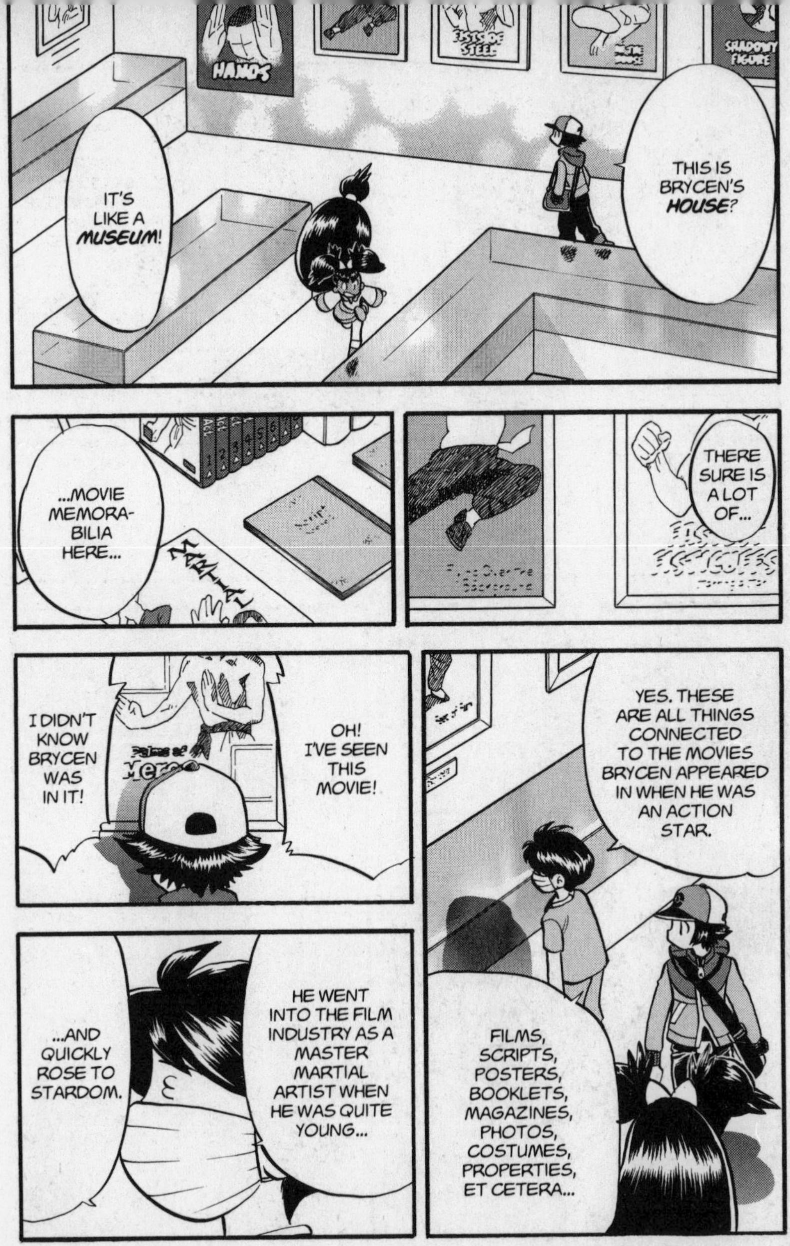
SHADOWY FIGURE
FISTS OF STEEL
HANDS
THIS IS BRYCEN'S *HOUSE*?
IT'S LIKE A *MUSEUM*!
THERE SURE IS A LOT OF...
...MOVIE MEMORABILIA HERE...
MARTIAL
YES. THESE ARE ALL THINGS CONNECTED TO THE MOVIES BRYCEN APPEARED IN WHEN HE WAS AN ACTION STAR.
FILMS, SCRIPTS, POSTERS, BOOKLETS, MAGAZINES, PHOTOS, COSTUMES, PROPERTIES, ET CETERA...
OH! I'VE SEEN THIS MOVIE!
I DIDN'T KNOW BRYCEN WAS IN IT!
HE WENT INTO THE FILM INDUSTRY AS A MASTER MARTIAL ARTIST WHEN HE WAS QUITE YOUNG...
...AND QUICKLY ROSE TO STARDOM.

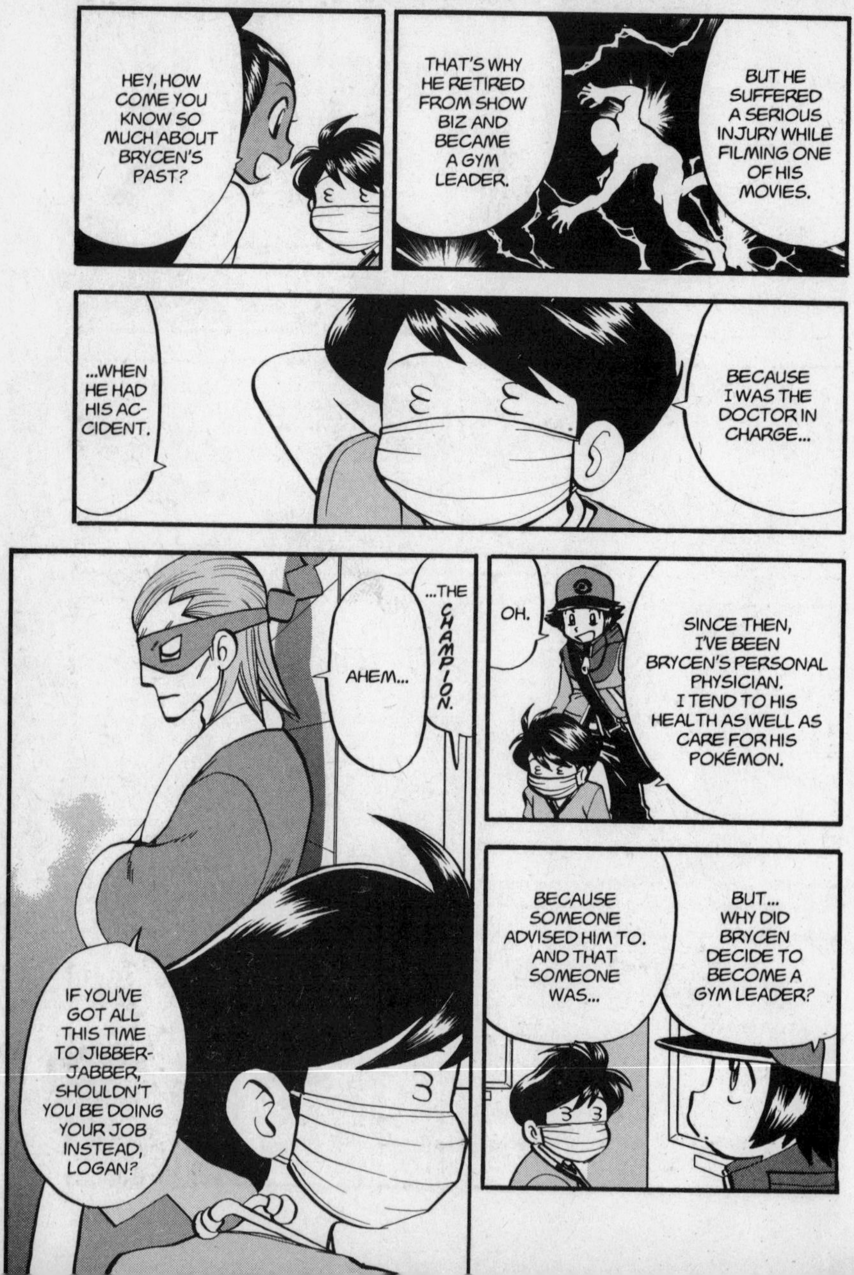
BUT HE SUFFERED A SERIOUS INJURY WHILE FILMING ONE OF HIS MOVIES.
THAT'S WHY HE RETIRED FROM SHOW BIZ AND BECAME A GYM LEADER.
HEY, HOW COME YOU KNOW SO MUCH ABOUT BRYCEN'S PAST?
BECAUSE I WAS THE DOCTOR IN CHARGE...
...WHEN HE HAD HIS AC-CIDENT.
SINCE THEN, I'VE BEEN BRYCEN'S PERSONAL PHYSICIAN. I TEND TO HIS HEALTH AS WELL AS CARE FOR HIS POKÉMON.
OH.
BUT... WHY DID BRYCEN DECIDE TO BECOME A GYM LEADER?
BECAUSE SOMEONE ADVISED HIM TO. AND THAT SOMEONE WAS...
...THE CHAMPION.
AHEM...
IF YOU'VE GOT ALL THIS TIME TO JIBBER-JABBER, SHOULDN'T YOU BE DOING YOUR JOB INSTEAD, LOGAN?

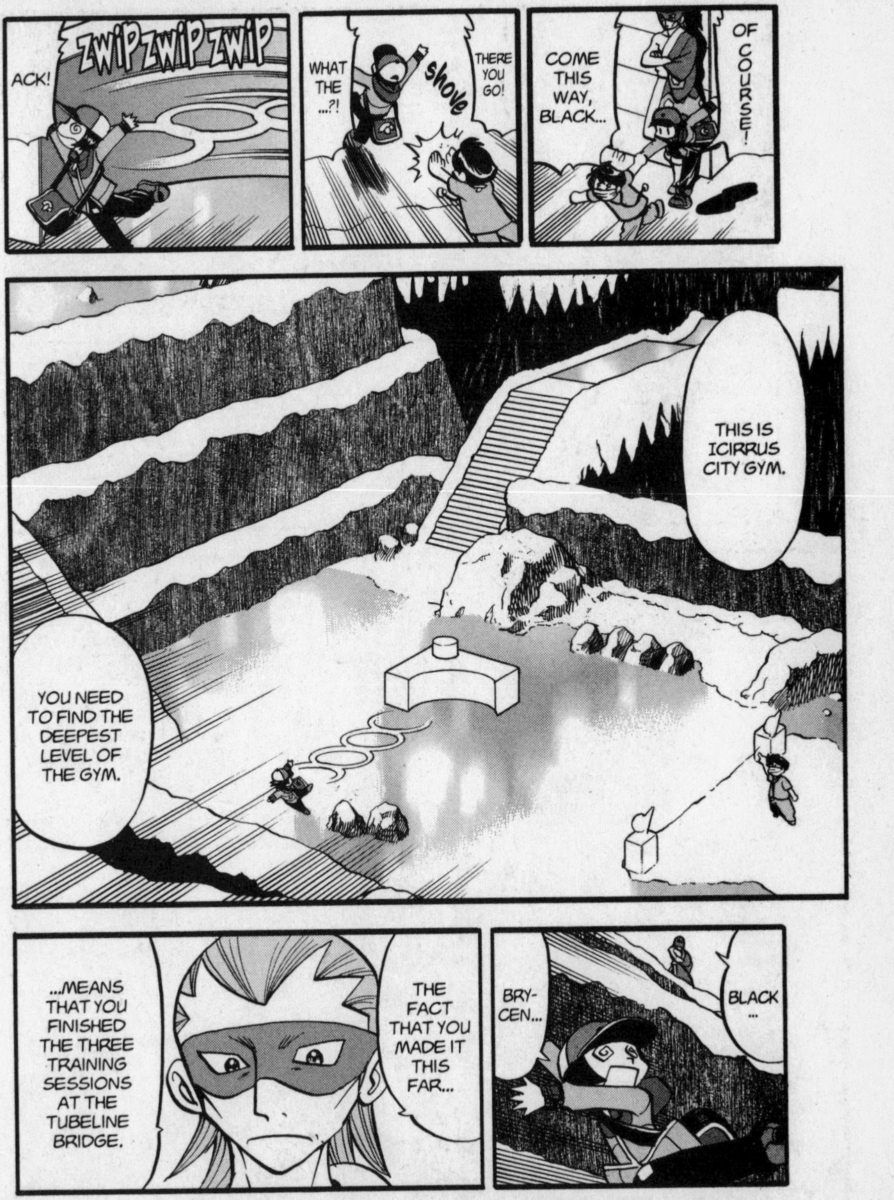
OF COURSE!
COME THIS WAY, BLACK...
THERE YOU GO!
shove
WHAT THE ...?!
ZWIP ZWIP ZWIP
ACK!
THIS IS ICIRRUS CITY GYM.
YOU NEED TO FIND THE DEEPEST LEVEL OF THE GYM.
BLACK ...
BRY-CEN...
THE FACT THAT YOU MADE IT THIS FAR...
...MEANS THAT YOU FINISHED THE THREE TRAINING SESSIONS AT THE TUBELINE BRIDGE.

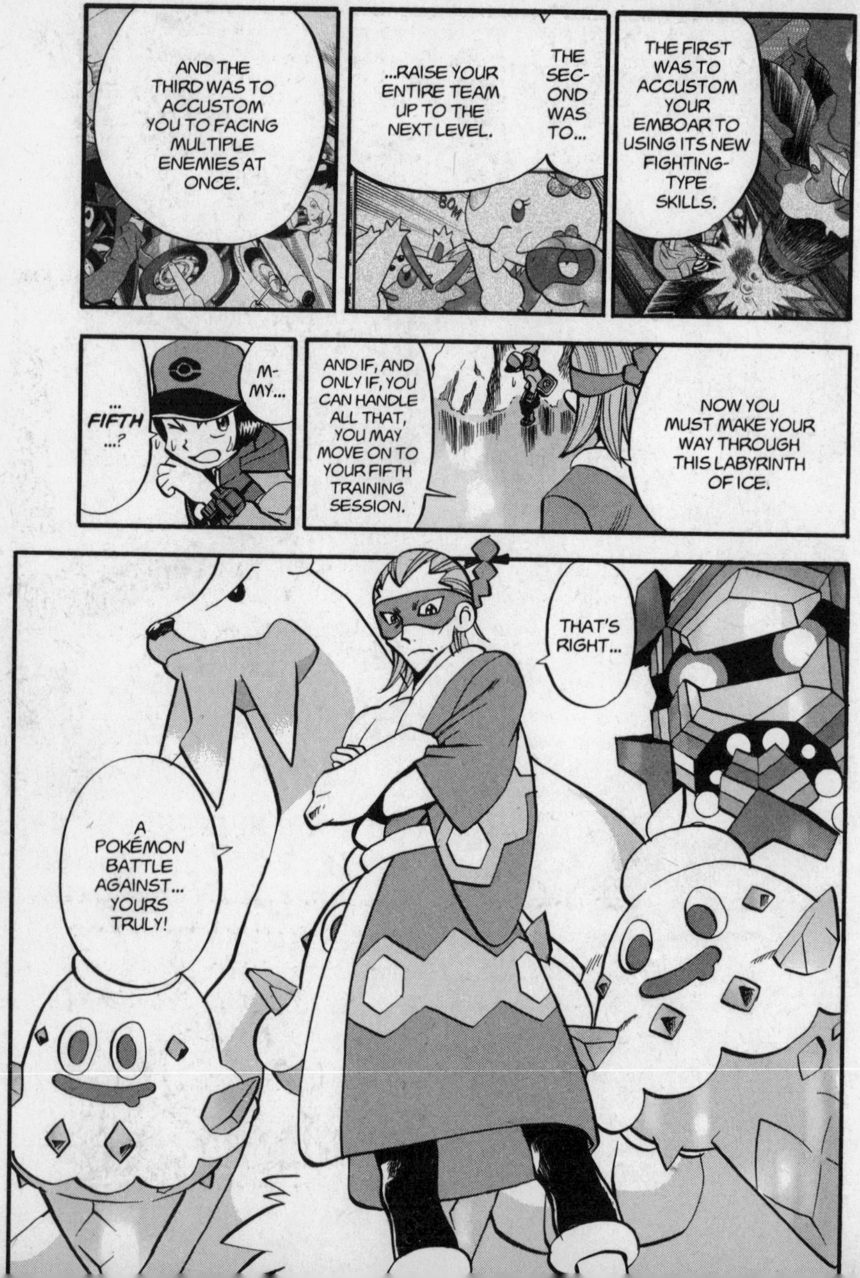
THE FIRST WAS TO ACCUSTOM YOUR EMBOAR TO USING ITS NEW FIGHTING-TYPE SKILLS.
THE SEC-OND WAS TO...
...RAISE YOUR ENTIRE TEAM UP TO THE NEXT LEVEL.
BOM
AND THE THIRD WAS TO ACCUSTOM YOU TO FACING MULTIPLE ENEMIES AT ONCE.
NOW YOU MUST MAKE YOUR WAY THROUGH THIS LABYRINTH OF ICE.
AND IF, AND ONLY IF, YOU CAN HANDLE ALL THAT, YOU MAY MOVE ON TO YOUR FIFTH TRAINING SESSION.
M-MY...
...FIFTH...?
THAT'S RIGHT...
A POKÉMON BATTLE AGAINST... YOURS TRULY!

More Adventures COMING SOON...

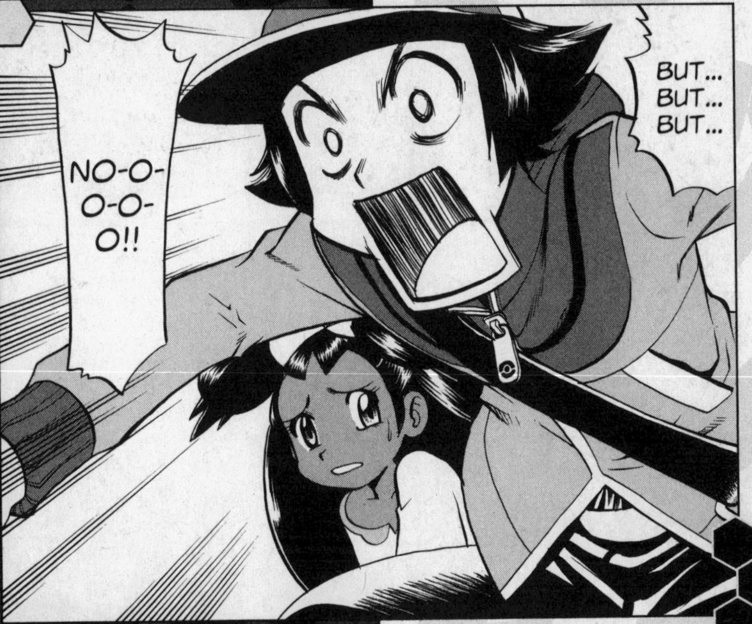
BUT... BUT... BUT...
NO-O-O-O-O-O!!

Black is training hard with Gym Leaders Drayden and Brycen so he can help rescue the other Gym Leaders from the clutches of Team Plasma... But what are his new mentors planning to ask of him? And is it something he is willing—or able—to do? Also, Black learns a secret about his archenemy, mysterious N of Team Plasma!

THEN—OH NO! IS IT TOO LATE FOR BLACK TO QUALIFY FOR THE POKÉMON LEAGUE?!

Plus, get to know and hang out with Cryogonal, Patrat, Vanillish, Beartic, Druddigon and...*Carracosta*?!

VOL. 14 AVAILABLE FEBRUARY 2014!

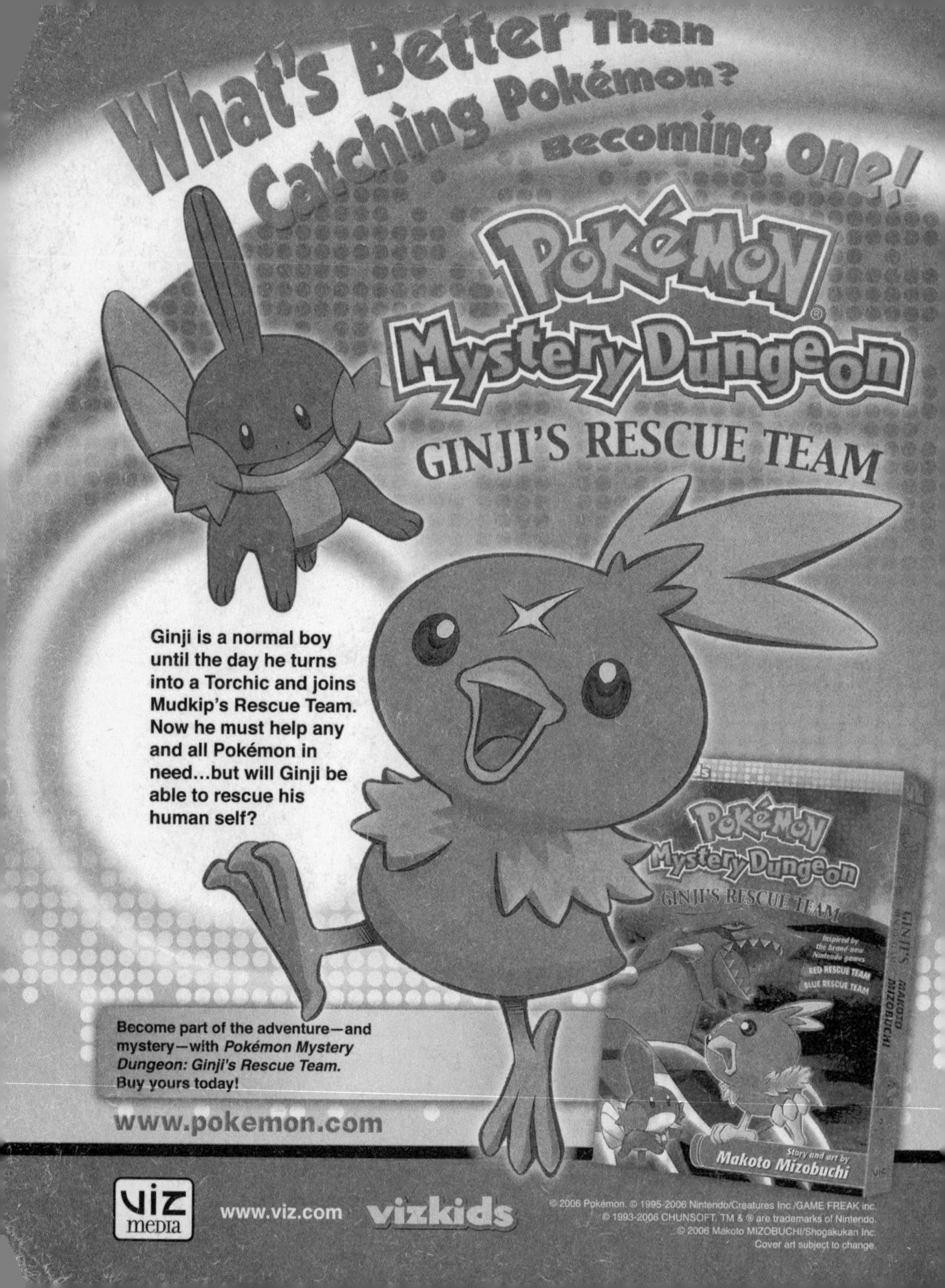
What's Better Than Catching Pokémon?
Becoming one!
Pokémon Mystery Dungeon
GINJI'S RESCUE TEAM
Ginji is a normal boy until the day he turns into a Torchic and joins Mudkip's Rescue Team. Now he must help any and all Pokémon in need...but will Ginji be able to rescue his human self?
Become part of the adventure—and mystery—with Pokémon Mystery Dungeon: Ginji's Rescue Team. Buy yours today!
www.pokemon.com
Pokémon Mystery Dungeon
GINJI'S RESCUE TEAM
Inspired by the brand-new Nintendo games
RED RESCUE TEAM
BLUE RESCUE TEAM
Story and art by Makoto Mizobuchi
viz media
www.viz.com
vizkids
© 2006 Pokémon. © 1995-2006 Nintendo/Creatures Inc./GAME FREAK inc.
© 1993-2006 CHUNSOFT. TM & ® are trademarks of Nintendo.
© 2006 Makoto MIZOBUCHI/Shogakukan Inc.
Cover art subject to change.

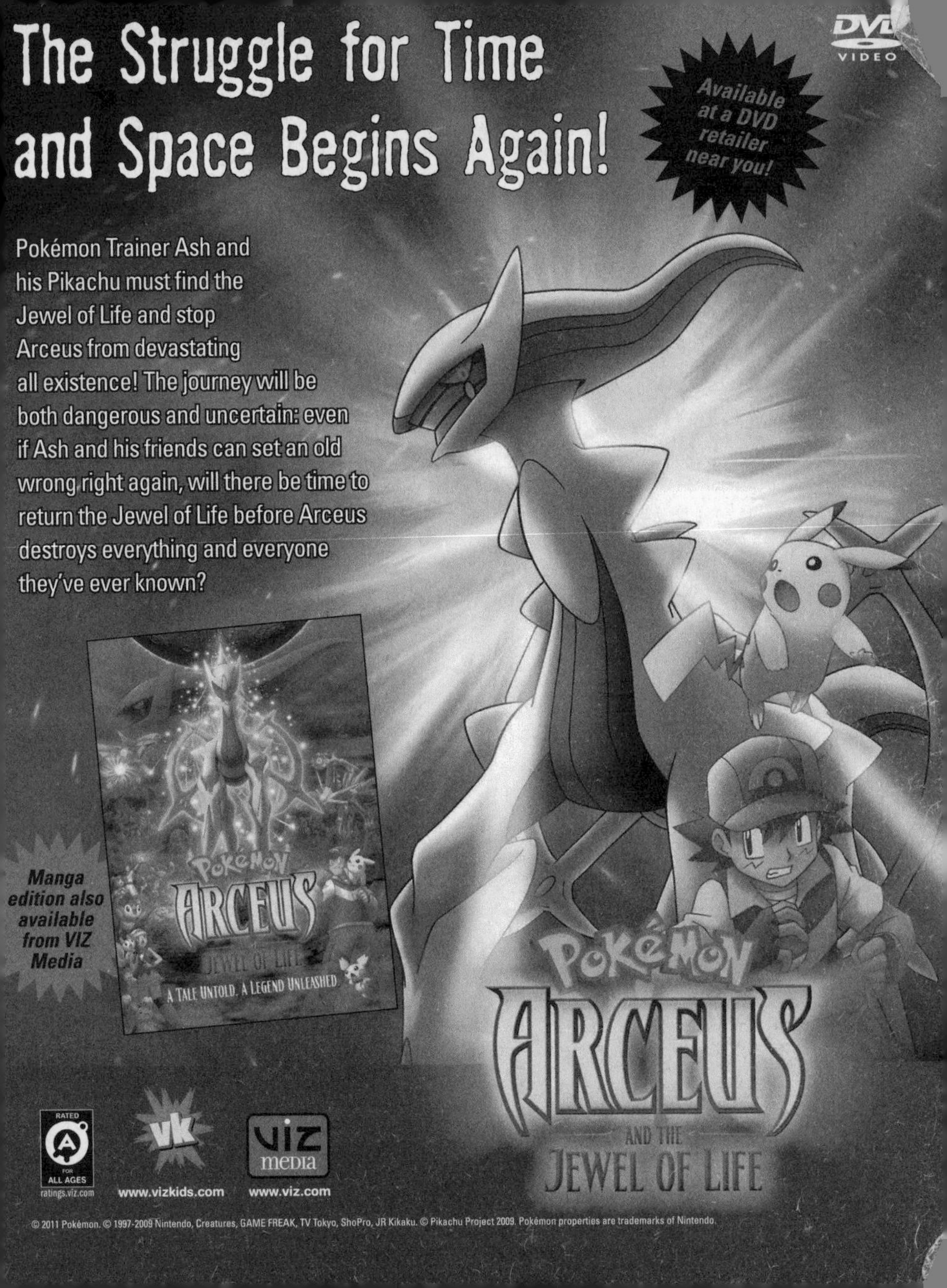
The Struggle for Time and Space Begins Again!
DVD VIDEO
Available at a DVD retailer near you!
Pokémon Trainer Ash and his Pikachu must find the Jewel of Life and stop Arceus from devastating all existence! The journey will be both dangerous and uncertain: even if Ash and his friends can set an old wrong right again, will there be time to return the Jewel of Life before Arceus destroys everything and everyone they've ever known?
Pokémon Arceus Jewel of Life
A Tale Untold, A Legend Unleashed
Manga edition also available from VIZ Media
Pokémon Arceus and the Jewel of Life
RATED A FOR ALL AGES
ratings.viz.com
vk
www.vizkids.com
viz media
www.viz.com
© 2011 Pokémon. © 1997-2009 Nintendo, Creatures, GAME FREAK, TV Tokyo, ShoPro, JR Kikaku. © Pikachu Project 2009. Pokémon properties are trademarks of Nintendo.

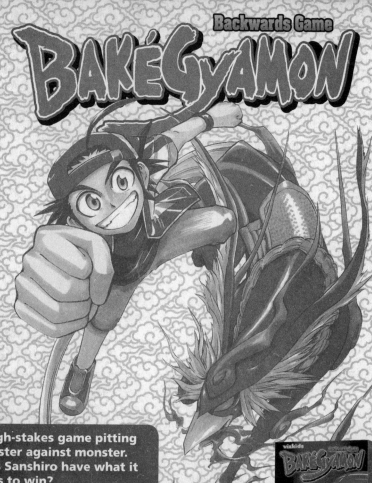

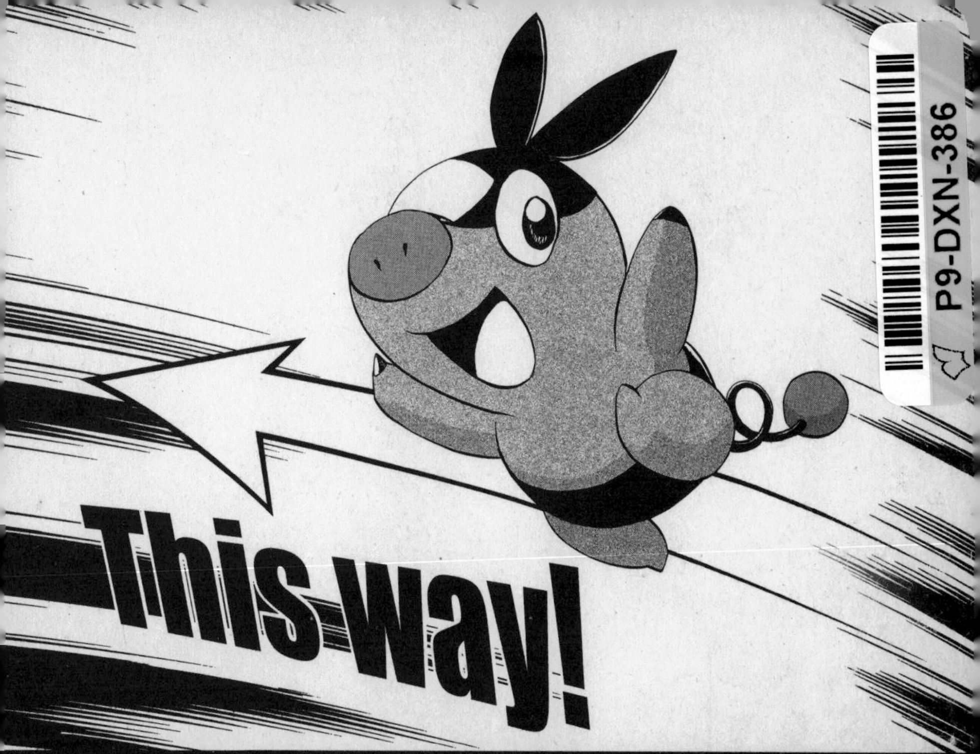
This way!

THIS IS THE END OF THIS GRAPHIC NOVEL!

To properly enjoy this VIZ Media graphic novel, please turn it around and begin reading from right to left.

This book has been printed in the original Japanese format in order to preserve the orientation of the original artwork. Have fun with it!

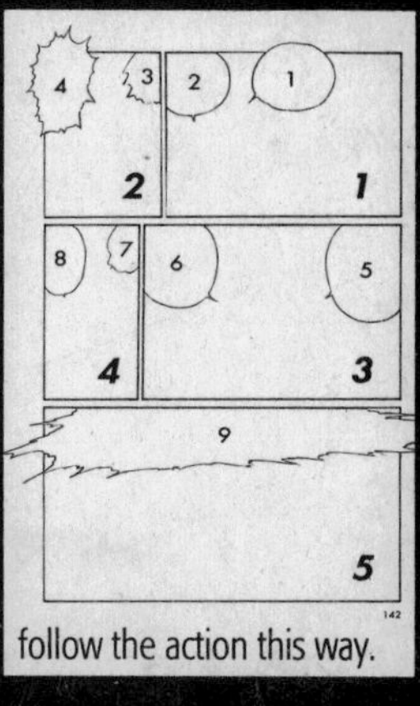
1
2
3
4
5
follow the action this way.